JUROR 11

A Story of Murder A Story of Judgment

JUROR 11

A Story of Murder A Story of Judgment

Terry Allen Rathmann

A Shepherd's Life 7 INC.
www.ashepherdslife.org

All names have been changed to protect the innocent…and the guilty.

Juror 11 - A Story of Murder - A Story of Judgment
2nd edition
Copyright © 2016 by Terry Rathmann

Published by A Shepherd's Life 7 INC.
First published in July 2015
Visit www.ashepherdslife.org for more information on how to live A Shepherds Life.

Rathmann, Terry
Juror 11 - A Story of Murder - A Story of Judgment
Includes bibliographical references

ISBN: 978-0-9861171-1-4
ISBN: 0-9861171-1-0
Library of Congress Control Number: 2015908266
Shepherd's Life, A Suwanee, GA

Cover designed by Julie Slappey with Crush Design Group. www.crushdg.com

This book is gratefully dedicated to my loving wife, Lynda Rathmann. Because you took on additional responsibilities at our business and at home, I had extra time to commit to writing. What a gift! Thank you for your support and encouragement. Lynda, I love you dearly!

Table of Contents

Introduction

Your Virtual Juror Instructions

Ever wanted to be a juror on an important trial? Now is your chance. In this book, you'll be a virtual juror, experiencing the challenges of a trial involving murder, deception, judgment and plenty of excitement. I was the foreperson of an actual murder trial, and I've brought the story to you – although names in this book have been changed and some information supplemented. While based on an actual court case, I have taken the liberty in telling this story of introducing fictional characters in an effort to provide some explanation behind what might have motivated juror 6. Any resemblance to real persons, living or dead, is purely coincidental.

Don't skip ahead! Knowing the end result will not give you any benefits. Instead, it will take away the challenge of sitting in the jury panel box as you seek the truth and decide if the defendant is guilty or innocent.

In the past few years, a variety of murders have captured our nation's attention. Many times, uninvolved people are quick to indict the accused, often within hours of the incident. Politicians take the microphone and the rest of us turn to social media to proclaim our horror and expound on the guilt of the accused. Keeping our impartiality is no easy task.

Juror 11 does not attempt to explain why justice sometimes prevails while at other times it seems nowhere to be found. Instead, Juror 11 offers you a chance to experience the judicial process as a virtual juror who ultimately must judge a fellow citizen.

Knowing yourself, can you consider someone innocent until proven guilty? Knowing yourself, can you be a fair and impartial juror and base your judgment on the facts of the case? If you believe you can, then take the Juror 11 Pledge, and let's get started!

Take The Virtual Juror Member Oath

"You shall, well and truly, try the issues formed upon the Bill of Indictment between the State of Georgia and Mr. Darren Paulson. Mr. Paulson is charged with the offenses of murder, felony murder, aggravated assault, and possession of a firearm during the commission of a felony. You shall give the true verdict according to the evidence that you receive, so help you God. Please state 'I will.'"

YOUR VIRTUAL JUROR MEMBER VERDICT FORM

WE THE JURY FIND THE DEFENDANT AS TO:

Count 1 – Murder
_____Guilty or _____Not Guilty
Or
Lesser included offense of Voluntary Manslaughter
_____Guilty or _____Not Guilty

Count 2 – Felony Murder
_____Guilty or _____Not Guilty
Or
Lesser included offense of Voluntary Manslaughter
_____Guilty or _____Not Guilty

Count 3 – Aggravated Assault

_____Guilty or _____Not Guilty

Count 4 – Possession of Firearm during Commission of Felony

_____Guilty or _____Not Guilty

Count 5 – Possession of Firearm during Commission of Felony

_____Guilty or _____Not Guilty

Count 6 – Possession of Firearm during Commission of Felony

_____Guilty or _____Not Guilty

Virtual Juror Member Signature: _____

Date: _____

Placement of main characters and some of the evidence submitted in the murder trial.

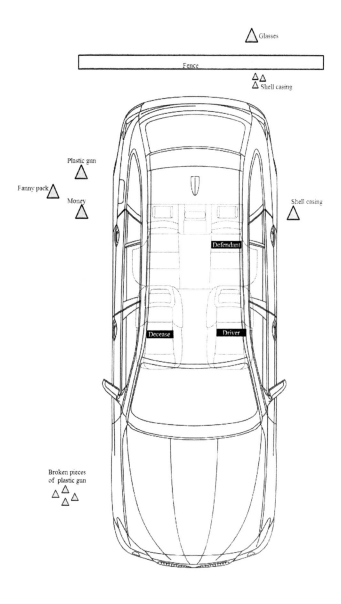

The characters of Juror 11

The bailiff	Steven Adams
The judge	Sandra Worthington
The defendant	Darren Paulson
The driver	Jared McDonald
The victim	Bob Candlestick
The defense attorney	Tim Edwin
The prosecutor	Thomas Albert
The son of the defendant's girlfriend	Joshua
The driver's cousin	Don Duffey
1st attorney for the defendant	Floyd Lovely
Juror 11	Terry Rathmann
Juror 6	Mary Davis
Mary's husband	Ricky Davis
Mary's son	Bobby
Mary's daughter	Cary
Mary's deceased younger brother	Andy
Mary's best friend	Janet
Mary's mother	Julie

Witnesses:

1st police officer on the scene	Jason Roberts
The driver	Jared McDonald
Officer who collected evidence	Alicia Zillow
Employee who found the money	Roal Ford
Supervisor of the defendant	Raymond Hunter
Lead investigator – detective	Jon Godskeep
Medical examiner	Patti Filzen
Medical investigator	Lyle Mielke
The defendant	Darren Paulson
The driver's uncle	Scott Target
Private investigator	Greg Bar

Additional Jury Members:

Judy Mann	Anne Dikhouphiphet
Marilyn Schneider	Marvin Goodson
Ron Frost	Steve Christopher
Sam Nichols	Sang Martinez
Rosemary Bonine	Shelby Clinton

Chapter One

Innocent Until Proven Guilty

Can you, or anyone else for that matter, be fair and impartial when asked to judge other human beings? Recently, I was interviewed by CBS46 in Atlanta regarding the Justin Ross Harris trial after the judge granted a change of venue. The trial was moved from Cobb County, Georgia, in April 2016 because of the difficulty of finding enough impartial jurors to proceed locally.

I will give you more details about that interview a little later in the book, but first, please consider these questions. Do you think justice in the American court system is possible? Do you think the legal system is flawed and can be tilted one way or another? Do you think the term 'balancing the scales of justice' is just wishful thinking? Do you think attorneys attempt to seek the truth, or do they just want to win the case no matter the collateral damage?

Have you ever been seated in a juror panel box for a significant trial? Do you think it is possible for a juror who has an unresolved issue from his or her past to possess a desire to tilt the scales of justice and influence a verdict?

Do you think a juror who thinks he or she has been dealt a bad hand in the game of life might attempt to get even with society after being granted supreme power over another person's life during a trial? Do you think a juror might use that power to avenge something or someone?

Do you think the American court system is flawed because the system uses human beings, who are themselves flawed? Have you ever asked yourself who judges the jury during and after a highly publicized trial?

Before serving on a jury, I never really put much consideration into how many of our daily decisions are controlled by our beliefs and values. I didn't realize that my personal beliefs control the way I make the most significant decisions about my life and the lives of my family members.

Prior to this trial I didn't comprehend how much I was influenced by the schools I attended, the businesses that employed me, and the television shows that I watched. I also never quite realized how the people I associated with, including my extended family, impact the way I process information when evaluating a situation or a person.

In January of 2010, I was summoned to report to the Gwinnett County Courthouse for jury duty. I was reluctant. My wife and I work together running a small business, and although we have several employees, when one of us is absent, there is a heavier workload for the others.

At the courthouse, I found myself in a large holding room with hundreds of potential jurors. We were instructed by county employees to look for our name on the jumbo screens. My name appeared, indicating that I had been selected to follow Steven Adams, the court-appointed bailiff.

In a courtroom filled with potential jurors, the judge presiding over the case explained that the selected 12 jurors would be responsible for reviewing the presented evidence and listening to witnesses in a murder case that had happened several years earlier.

The term *voir dire* [**vwahr deer**; *French* vwar **deer**] is derived from a Latin term that basically means "to speak the truth." It refers to the process by which prospective jurors are questioned about their backgrounds and potential biases and prejudices before being selected to sit on a jury. The term also refers to the process by which witnesses are questioned about their background and qualifications before being allowed to present their testimony as subject experts in a court of law.

Before I had the opportunity to experience *voir dire*, I – along with the other prospective jurors – had to raise my right hand and take the two oaths administered by Judge Sandra Worthington. The first: "Ladies and gentlemen of the jury, you shall well truly try, that each case that's submitted to you during this present term of Court, and a true verdict give, according to the law which will be given you in the charge and the opinion that you entertain of the evidence that's produced to you to the best of your skill and knowledge, without favor or affection to either party, so help you God. If so, say I will." In unison, the prospective jurors said "I will," and the judge then instructed us to keep our hands up for the next oath.

"You shall give true answers to all questions as may be asked by the Court or its authority, including all questions asked by the parties or their attorneys concerning your qualifications as jurors in the case of the State of Georgia versus Darren Paulson, so help you God."

A tsunami of emotions swept over me as I realized how serious this legal process was for Paulson, who was being charged with murder and five other felony offenses. The judge informed us that this trial could take more than a week and that the questions the attorneys were about to ask us would be quite personal.

The prosecuting attorney asked me if I had ever taken self-defense classes or if I had ever been in a situation where I was afraid that someone would physically harm me. He asked me if I had ever lost anyone close to me, if I thought it was okay to use a weapon to defend myself, if I owned a hand gun, and if I had ever been in the military or had a job as a police officer.

The prosecuting attorney asked me if I had ever been arrested, and if so, did I feel I was treated fairly? He asked me about my family and if there had been anyone with drug or alcohol addictions. He asked if

I was able – both emotionally and physically – to view graphic photographs. I was asked about the schools I attended and what type of jobs I had during my lifetime. Finally, he asked me if I had ever personally met the defendant, the prosecuting attorney, the defense attorney, or the judge presiding over the trial.

Then I was asked several questions by the defense attorney that have caused me to spend countless hours pondering how well I know myself: "Knowing yourself, is there any reason you can think of that would require Mr. Paulson to present evidence to prove his innocence? Knowing yourself, is there any reason that you could not wait until all the evidence is admitted and this Honorable Court presents the charges on the law before you make your decision about this case? Knowing yourself, do you believe you would have trouble keeping an open mind about this case until after you heard all the evidence? Knowing yourself, can you look at Mr. Paulson as being innocent until proven guilty?"

I could not think of any reason at that moment that would prevent me from looking at the defendant as being innocent until proven guilty. But as the defense attorney moved on to ask a series of similar questions to another prospective juror, I began to question myself, and my answers. Do I truly look at people as being innocent until proven guilty, and until I have heard all of the facts about the challenges they might be facing? I began to reflect on the term "knowing yourself" and began wondering if I truly knew myself in terms of my current biases, prejudices and emotional intelligence.

I actually could remember a time when I jumped to a conclusion about a person's ability and character, based upon my own faulty belief system. That time, I made a judgment call without making an effort to talk directly with the person involved. It happened when I was a soldier in the United States Army Infantry. I was given a new squad leader, a man who had been an Army Ranger before reenlisting in the Army Infantry. For those who are not aware, an Army Ranger is specially trained to fight our country's adversaries at a moment's notice.

I had almost joined the Ranger Battalion after completing Basic Training and Airborne School. The recruiter put the contract in front of me, and I picked up a pen. However, as I went to sign the new agreement, a voice in my head told me to stick to my original plan. I didn't join the Rangers, I eventually completed my original tour, and I used the GI Bill to finance my college education.

So while in the Infantry, when I first looked at Sgt. Brett Mitchell, I wondered why he was no longer a Ranger. I wondered why he left the Army, became a civilian, and then signed an agreement to perform a tour in the Army Infantry. I thought perhaps he couldn't cut it as a Ranger, and perhaps he could not make it as a civilian. Now, I thought with suspicion, this man was going to be my squad leader!

Well, my initial judgment was flat-out wrong. I learned more about survival from Sgt. Mitchell than from anyone else during my time in the Army. His leadership skills were unmatched. I can honestly say that there have been only a few people in my life who I would die for, and Sgt. Mitchell was one of them.

The gravity of my responses to the defense attorney hit me like a boulder. Did I really believe the answers I gave under oath? Did I speak the truth, or did I simply answer the questions in the way I consider myself to be – and the way I want others to see me?

Listening to the attorneys ask similar questions of everyone in the potential jury pool, I could tell that they were searching for people who could be open-minded, fair and impartial. It also became very apparent to me that the attorneys had a complete understanding of how our life experiences can impact the way we think. Based on the answers to certain questions, they could get a sense about individuals, and determine if their biases were leaning in favor of Paulson and the defense attorney or toward the views of the prosecuting attorney.

While the attorneys were quietly working together, accepting and rejecting the potential jurors sitting in the courtroom, the judge gave us a refresher course on our legal system.

"Under the Constitution of the United States," she began, "we say every person has the right to a jury trial of his or her peers, so we want that jury to reflect the county at large. The jury panel should be reflective of the population of the county's residents. A jury's verdict is meant to be the voice of the community. The Founding Fathers decided that people should have a voice and be able to give input in their government. Citizens can do this by registering to vote, and then actually voting to elect the people who establish the laws and preside over the government. If you do not like what you see in your government representation, then you have the ability to change that representation by casting your vote for another candidate when the time comes."

I have always been fascinated by how our government was formed and how citizens have the ability to provide input – in fact, I have a political science degree from the University of Central Florida – so I truly enjoyed the judge's reminder of our country's history. The judge concluded her background remarks by saying, "Our Founding Fathers truly believed in a tripartite government that consists of the executive, the judiciary, and the legislative branches. They believed that our judiciary system should be held somewhat accountable to the citizens of the country it rules. They wanted decisions to reflect the will of the community, and while there are legal standards, those standards are to be decided by the people of the community as well.

"A government should be created, as Abraham Lincoln said in the last part of the Gettysburg Address during the Civil War, that this nation, under God, shall have a new birth of freedom—and that government of the people, by the people, for the people, shall not perish from the earth."

At this point, reminded that we truly live in the best country in the world, I could feel my pride of being an American swell inside me. I remembered the Army values of Loyalty, Duty, Respect, Selfless Service, Honor, Integrity, and Personal Courage. Making the decision to live up to these values is a commitment every American should make.

After the attorneys concluded their conversation, the Clerk of Courts called out the names of 14 individuals – 12 jurors to deliberate the evidence submitted in court and two alternates, who would deliberate the case if or when one of the original 12 was unable to complete the trial.

The second name the clerk called out was Terry Rathmann – No. 11 – and I was thrilled to be selected. Despite the inconvenience on the home and work front, I was filled with civic and patriotic pride, and I was determined to be a fair and open-minded juror, seeking the truth only from the information that soon would be shared with all of us on the jury panel. I truly believed I would be able to view the defendant as innocent, unless proven guilty.

The judge then explained what to expect. "The next phase for the jury panel is to listen to the opening remarks from both attorneys. Their opening statements are not to be considered as evidence. Opening remarks are simply where the law allows the attorneys to outline their case to you, the jury. It's their opportunity to tell you what they expect this case to be about and what they expect the evidence will represent.

"Following the opening statements comes the evidentiary part of the trial, where the witnesses appear, and testify under oath as to the facts within their knowledge. Now, evidence can come to a jury in another way besides a witness' testimony, and that's what we refer to as documentary or physical evidence. This could be literally anything – any type of tangible object or book or paper, notebook, photograph, etc. If there is physical evidence, and it's admitted during the trial, generally it goes out with the jury to the room where deliberations occur." The judge paused for a moment to let her words sink in.

"Following the evidentiary part of the trial, we enter into what's called closing arguments. This is what we call the persuasion part of the trial. It's where the law specifically allows the attorneys to try to persuade you as to how they would like you to answer the charges listed on the official verdict form. It's their chance under the law to argue their case directly to you, the jury panel.

"Following the closing arguments, you will hear the charges posed against the defendant. This is where I, the trial judge, have the duty and responsibility to instruct you on what law it is that applies to this particular case. At the conclusion of the charge, you, the jurors, will leave to begin your deliberations, where you apply the facts as you find them to be, in regards to the law I have given you. You are each asked to reach a verdict that speaks the truth based on all you will have seen and heard." Again, she paused to give us a moment to consider her words.

"Now, it is very important that you don't make up your mind until you've heard all the evidence, the law that applies to that evidence, and your fellow jurors' opinions. So we ask you not to jump to any conclusions. Your job as a juror is kind of like a sponge; you're to sit back and soak everything up as well as you can, so that when it comes time to deliberate, you will have all the information you need to reach a verdict.

"It is also very important that you do not discuss the case with anyone during the trial or do any outside investigation on the case," she admonished. "Do not attempt to look up anything on the internet in regards to the people involved in this case, as well as any details of the murder itself. The evidence in this case comes from the courtroom, from witnesses' testimonies, and the exhibits admitted. That information is what you base your decision upon.

"If you hear about places and certain locations described during the trial, do not go out driving around and look at them, then come back and tell your fellow jurors. Again, the only evidence that you will be evaluating comes from this courtroom." The judge looked at us as we sat silently listening to her instructions.

"When it comes time to deliberate, you are instructed not to tweet any updates to anyone or post your thoughts on your Facebook page. Do not call your friends, text, or email any type of information that relates to this case. If you talk to somebody else about this case, it is human nature that they will not be able to resist telling you what to do or offer their insight and opinions on the case. Remember, only you as a collective body are sitting here and listening to everything. Only you really know what is said, and how it was said or presented, so we want the verdict to rest with you and no one else."

Chapter Two

Juror 6

Previously, I wrote about how our social, educational, and professional experiences help shape our personalities and our perceptions of reality. In addition, tragic and non-tragic events in our lives influence our behaviors, emotional responses and the type of lens that we use to view our world.

Before I entered the courthouse that Monday morning, I had never set eyes on juror 6. While my descriptions of her behaviors in the courthouse and jury deliberation room are accurate, I have supplemented those with fictional background information about her in an effort to determine her motivations.

Mary Davis came home from work on Wednesday evening around 6 p.m., parked her car in the garage, and then walked to the mailbox to retrieve the daily mail. As she returned to the garage, Mary spotted her son Bobby's bicycle lying in the neighbor's yard. Flipping through the mail as she entered the kitchen, she noticed a letter from the Gwinnett County Courthouse. Her children yelled down their greetings from upstairs, asking what was for dinner, as she opened the envelope.

Her mind on the letter, a summons for jury duty the following Monday, Mary called back, "Nothing until Bobby picks up his bike from the neighbor's yard and puts it back in the garage. Cary, you need to pick up your things from the living room, too!"

She put down the letter and removed two frozen pizzas from the freezer. Adding a salad and water to the night's menu, she prepared the table for four.

As Mary finished her preparations, her husband, Ricky, arrived. Mary told him dinner was almost ready and called to the kids to wash their hands and come to the table.

A few minutes later, everyone was seated, and Ricky instructed the family to bow their heads as he prayed, "Heavenly Father, thank you for this meal we are about to receive. Thank you for my family being of good health and all your blessings you bestow upon us, the ones that we see, as well as the blessings we do not always recognize. We ask you to protect us from harm and to keep our hearts pure and full of peace and love. In your precious Son's name, Jesus Christ, we pray, Amen."

Mary asked the children about school that day, and then asked Ricky how his day was at work. Everyone participated in the discussion and, after they finished telling their news of the day, Mary mentioned the letter she had received from the courthouse regarding jury duty. Always inquisitive for a 12-year-old, Bobby asked his mother several questions about the letter and why there was such a thing called jury duty. Mary explained the best she could, what is involved when people are selected to serve on a jury panel.

Finishing up the pizza, Ricky said, "Look at this as another adventure that God has given to you. And come Monday morning I'll make sure the kids are fed and on their way to school so you can be at the courthouse by 8. From what I've read, though, chances are slim that you will be assigned to a case. Many of the cases enter into a plea bargain by the attorneys before they ever go before a jury."

The rest of the week flew by quickly, and Mary had little chance to think about the jury summons. It wasn't until she and her family were attending church services on Sunday morning that her mind began to drift, and she mused a bit anxiously about the events of the next day.

Mary wondered if she might hear an important case or an interesting lawsuit and, despite her nervousness, she silently began to hope that she would be chosen for a jury trial.

Applause from the audience at the conclusion of the pastor's message brought Mary back to the present. Leaving the church, she ran into her best friend, Janet. Janet asked Mary if she was still fasting, since she and many others in their Bible Study group had agreed not to eat any meat for 30 days. Mary replied, "Yes, and we are all looking forward to the 30 days ending tomorrow!" They talked about the pastor's message for a few minutes, and then Mary told Janet that she had been summoned for jury duty the next morning.

Janet sighed. "What a burden that would be! If you don't want to get assigned, just tell the lawyers and the judge something about your past that might show a bias, or make something up. That way, you may get out of work for a day or two, but your week can go on as it normally does." Surprised and disappointed in Janet, Mary just nodded, but her anxiety about her summons to court grew.

Later that evening, Mary and Ricky said goodnight to their children. Although both Bobby and Cary were almost teen-agers, they still said the same evening prayer with them they had said since the children were first born: "Now I lay me down to sleep, I pray the Lord my soul to keep, if I die before I wake, I pray the Lord my soul to take. Amen."

In their own bedroom, Mary told her husband she was a little anxious about reporting for jury duty. Unlike Janet, Ricky stated that everything would work itself out. "Just let God and the Holy Spirit guide your heart, and whatever you do and say tomorrow will not be a big ordeal for you." Mary agreed, saying she would take one step at a time and let God be in charge.

The morning seemed to come too fast for Mary, and she felt rushed getting ready to leave for the courthouse. She couldn't stop thinking about all the different scenarios that could present themselves to her at jury duty, and she felt a combination of excitement and anxiety about the possibilities.

After arriving at the courthouse, Mary was seated in the large jury holding room. Only a few minutes passed before she saw her name on the big screen and was called to follow the bailiff. As Mary sat down in the courtroom, her excitement continued to mount as the possibility of being assigned to an important case drew near.

Like the other potential jury candidates, Mary was told by the judge that the trial would be about a person being killed by a gunshot. At that, Mary's heart began to pound in her chest. Twelve years previously, her younger brother Andy was shot and killed by a stray bullet in a movie theater parking lot. A fight had broken out on the other side of the lot, and shots were fired, but the shooters then left the scene – perhaps not even realizing they had killed someone. With only three more weeks of high school remaining, Andy had been planning to attend the Georgia Institute of Technology on an academic scholarship.

Mary, who had been married less than two years at the time, was devastated at the news that her brother was killed. The senseless death of her younger brother took a toll on her marriage as well as her relationship with God. Pregnant with Bobby, she could not understand why the murder of her brother Andy, had happened to her.

Mary's sadness permeated her days. Andy was not given a chance to live out his life and to fulfill any of the dreams he had shared with her. Her heart ached while her mind could not wrap itself around why this tragic event had to happen to her. It was incomprehensible that the people responsible could not be found and arrested, and that justice was never served.

Mary's reflections about her brother were cut short when the defense attorney turned to her, asking her the same questions he had asked so many other prospective jurors that morning.

Suddenly, Mary very much wanted to be on this jury panel. She deliberately did not tell either attorney about being involved in a police investigation or about the fact that there was an unsolved murder in her family's history. Mary knew that if she revealed Andy's murder to the attorneys, she would have only a slim chance of being selected as a juror. Keeping her answers short, she asked God to forgive her for not speaking the truth.

Later that afternoon, having been selected to the jury panel, Mary slowly drove home from the courthouse. She thought about how she would explain to her children that she now possessed the authority to consider a man guilty or innocent of killing someone. And, she knew, it would be even harder to explain to Ricky how she had been chosen for the jury in the first place. She knew her husband would never condone her deliberate lies to the attorneys, so she decided to be as vague as possible when discussing the case with him. She also decided she would tell Ricky what the judge had repeatedly said to the jurors about not discussing any part of the case with anyone. This warning included their spouses, because the judge said it was human nature for husbands and wives to provide their thoughts and possibly their verdicts of guilt or innocence.

Mary felt confident that she could hide her deception from Ricky, but she knew deep within her heart that she couldn't hide from God. Although she knew God would forgive her, she realized there might be consequences for her actions. Those, however, would be a small price to pay so that she could sit in the jury box and be part of this murder trial.

Pulling into the driveway, Mary could not remember the last time she had dreaded having a conversation with Ricky, but today she was grateful she had made it home before her husband. She opened the door to find both of her children waiting to hear about what had happened at the courthouse. As she started to prepare dinner, she explained to them that she was selected to sit on the jury panel, and that the attorneys would present evidence about what happened the night the defendant shot and killed a man.

Bobby's and Cary's jaws dropped, and their eyes widened. Bobby said, "You're going to be in a murder trial? Wait until I tell everyone at school!" and he and his 10-year-old sister rushed upstairs to text their friends.

Mary had just finished making spaghetti when Ricky arrived home. He called upstairs for the kids to wash up and come to the dinner table, where he gave thanks to the Lord for the meal they were about to receive. As they passed around the garlic bread, Bobby couldn't hold in his excitement. "Did Mommy tell you what happened at the courthouse today? Did she tell you that she is going to be a juror in a murder trial? Isn't that cool, Dad?"

Ricky looked at his children and then at his wife in surprise. "Is that true?" he asked her.

Mary replied, "Yes, it is. The trial will start sometime tomorrow morning."

"Did the judge or the attorneys ask you any questions during the *voir dire* process?" Ricky asked in puzzlement.

Mary replied, "Yes, they did."

Ricky was finding Mary's short answers exasperating. "Can you elaborate? What did they ask you? And what did you respond?"

Mary said, "Honey, the judge said that we cannot talk about the trial to anyone, including our family, in fear that someone might say something that might impact what a jury panel member would think about the case."

Ricky fought the desire to ask more probing questions, but thought it unwise to do so in front of the children at the dinner table. However, as soon as Bobby and Cary were in bed, and he and Mary had retired to their own bedroom, he began asking his wife for details.

Uneasily, Mary said, "What do you want to know?"

Ricky sighed. "I want to know how you are going to be on a jury panel in a murder case when your brother Andy was murdered a dozen years ago. Didn't the attorneys care that you have an unresolved murder in your immediate family?"

"I guess it didn't really matter to them," Mary replied.

Ricky shook his head. "It is hard for me to imagine that they would not think it mattered that your baby brother was shot and killed. I could understand if this was a lawsuit over an estate or a DUI type of trial, but a murder trial? I would assume that they would have eliminated you from the jury pool right from the beginning."

Mary looked away. "Ricky, I can't explain their decisions. The entire questioning and answering session only took a few minutes. Please remember, I was ordered by the judge not to discuss the trial."

Again, Ricky shook his head. He had a bad feeling about Mary's short answers, and he couldn't help but think she was not telling him the truth. "The trial has not even started yet, so you can't use that as your excuse for not telling me what happened," he snapped. "I served on a jury, remember? And I know the process the attorneys use to select a jury panel that would either be neutral or perhaps even lean in their favor. Didn't they ask you about your past experiences dealing with law enforcement?"

Mary replied, "Yes, they did."

"Did you tell them how mad you were at the police department for not finding the people responsible for your brother's death?"

Mary knew that she could no longer be vague with her answers. She would either need to lie to her husband, or she would need to tell the whole truth about her desire to be a juror on this murder trial, no matter what. Mary gave herself one more second to evaluate her desire before she said with raised voice, "Yes, honey, I told them that I was frustrated with the process, and I told the attorneys I was frustrated that they never found the person who pulled the trigger that killed Andy."

Ricky's voice had grown louder, too. "Frustrated? You were more than frustrated. You were angry at everyone involved in the investigation. You took time yourself to talk to the people at the movie theater to try to find out if they saw a group of kids who regularly parked in the same area of the parking lot that night. You didn't believe the police department was competent. Mary, did you really only use the word 'frustrated' to describe how you felt?"

Mary replied, "Yes, that's the word I used."

Ricky sat on the bed and put his head in his hands. He shook his head back and forth, rubbed his eyes, and finally looked up at his wife.

"This doesn't make any sense to me," he said. "We both know you were much more than frustrated with the investigation. Heck, everyone around us – from your family to the place you worked, the people at our church – everyone knew you were much more than frustrated. Your anger almost tore us apart. Why would you use the word 'frustrated' to describe how you felt after your brother was killed? What are you not telling me?" He sighed and lowered his voice. "Mary, we said when we got married that we would be truthful to one another no matter what, but I have a terrible feeling inside that you're hiding something from me for some reason. So I am going to ask you flat out, honey, with God as our witness: Are you telling me everything that happened today?"

With her best reassuring glance, Mary replied, "Yes, honey, I am."

Mary went to bed that night with her heart aching. She could not remember ever lying to her husband, and she was aware that Ricky, tossing and turning beside her, knew she was lying. She loved him, respected him. A wonderful father to their two children, he was a hard-working man who led the family in a spiritual way. She hated deceiving him!

Mary began to pray to God, not just for forgiveness for her lies, but for His help to take away the tension between her and Ricky. She asked God to help protect their children from noticing the tension tomorrow morning as the family prepared for school and work.

But despite her turmoil, Mary felt she was mentally prepared to sit in the jury panel box to listen and ultimately judge the innocence or guilt of the defendant in a murder trial.

Chapter Three

Opening Statements

Upon my arrival at the courthouse, I found myself scanning the hundreds of people in the jury assembly room. I was wondering if any of them had been assigned to a murder case yesterday like I had been. My thoughts were interrupted by Mary, juror 6, who asked me, "Have you ever been a part of a murder trial before?"

I shook my head. "No, I have not."

Mary said she had never been selected to a jury panel either, but her husband, Ricky, had been chosen for a jury a few years back. She said he hadn't necessarily enjoyed the entire process, however.

"I don't remember all the details, but the trial was about a contract dispute between two business owners," Mary explained. "I believe the most difficult part for Ricky was when the jury members were deliberating the facts of the case. Again, I don't remember the details because it happened several years ago, but I think he mentioned that the 12 members of the jury panel had a difficult time agreeing on the verdict. I do remember him saying that he learned a lot about our legal system and the potential behavior of people placed in a stressful and foreign environment."

I was about to ask Mary another question when Adams, the bailiff, told us to follow him. My thoughts quickly turned back to the trial, and my excitement grew as we walked into the courtroom, and I took a seat in the jury box.

The judge wasted no time. "Ladies and gentlemen of the jury, we are ready to begin with the trial for this case. Before the attorneys make their opening statements, there's one last oath that we ask you to take, now that you have actually been seated as our trial jury. So I am going to ask all of you to raise your right hands and take the following oath:

"You shall well and truly, try the issues formed upon the Bill of Indictment between the State of Georgia and Mr. Darren Paulson. Mr. Paulson is charged with the offenses of murder, felony murder, aggravated assault, and possession of a firearm during the commission of a felony, and give the true verdict according to the evidence that you receive, so help you God. Please state I will."

I replied with conviction, "I will."

The next person to speak was Thomas Albert, the prosecuting attorney. When Albert was questioning me the day before during the *voir dire* process, he seemed to be a pleasant man with a job that I truly would not want to have. I can't imagine being an assistant district attorney and dealing on a daily basis with felony cases like sexual assaults, homicides, stabbings, shootings, burglaries, and drug and gun possessions.

Albert began the trial by stating, "Good morning. I always like to start with a little good news, and the good news is that opening statements are usually quick. With that said, the reason the judge told you that the words I am sharing with you now are called statements and not arguments is because at this point in the trial, there's nothing to argue about. All I can do on behalf of the State of Georgia is to make statements about what I believe the evidence is going to show you. This is not a whodunit type of murder mystery trial. We already know that Mr. Darren Paulson, the defendant, is the man who pulled the trigger that killed the victim, Mr. Bob Candlestick. Mr. Paulson openly admits to being the trigger man."

The last statement shed some light on what type of trial I was involved in. As part of the jury panel, we were not going to have to figure out who the shooter was in this case. I wrote down on the yellow notepad that had been supplied to me by the court that the defendant had already confessed to shooting the victim.

"I'm going to read through the felony charges listed in the Bill of Indictment, just to make sure everyone understands all the details of the indictment," Albert continued. "Count 1 charges Mr. Paulson with the offense of murder. Count 2 charges the defendant with the offense of felony murder, and it reads that the accused unlawfully, with malice, and aforethought caused the death of Mr. Candlestick by shooting him in the chest.

"Count 3 accuses Mr. Paulson of committing the offense of aggravated assault, and that he did, then and there, unlawfully make an assault upon the person of Mr. Candlestick with a handgun by shooting him in the chest. Counts 4, 5, and 6 are all related to the first three counts, charging Mr. Paulson with an offense called possession of a firearm during the commission of a felony. Count 4 is tied to count 1, the murder charge. Count 5 is tied to count 2, the felony murder charge, and Count 6 is linked to Count 3, which is the offense of aggravated assault."

I was writing furiously on my yellow notepad about the different charges and how some were linked to the different counts listed in the Bill of Indictment. The prosecuting attorney was speaking faster than I could write, however, and I started to feel overloaded, unable to absorb all of the information he was giving us. I wished I had the functionality of a DVR so I could pause and rewind what the prosecutor was saying. But as quickly as that thought appeared, it disappeared, for Albert was continuing with his opening statement.

"And that frames the issue that we're here for today, but it still doesn't tell you a lot of details about what happened the night in question. There is another person involved in this murder trial, and his name is Jared McDonald. Mr. McDonald was the driver of the car where Mr. Candlestick was shot and killed. Mr. McDonald knew the defendant, Mr. Paulson, through a relationship that he'd had with Mr. McDonald's cousin.

"When Mr. Paulson would hang out with his friend, occasionally Mr. McDonald would be present, so he had known him for about 10 years. In fact, I believe the evidence will show that he had actually purchased marijuana from Mr. Paulson in the past. Mr. Paulson didn't know Mr. Candlestick, but Mr. Candlestick did know Mr. McDonald. So it turns out that Mr. McDonald was the commonality among the three main people involved in this trial.

"Mr. Candlestick met Mr. McDonald at a barbershop while they were getting their hair cut, about a month before the shooting occurred. Evidently, they talked, and Mr. Candlestick asked Mr. McDonald if he knew where he could get some 'green,' some marijuana, in other words. Mr. McDonald said he thought he did, so he was the middleman, for lack of a better term. Mr. McDonald decided to contact Mr. Paulson about buying marijuana, and that he would drive Mr. Candlestick to meet with Mr. Paulson. What you are going to hear is that this was a drug deal – a drug deal gone bad, terribly bad."

I was sitting in the back row of the jury box when I saw Marvin, who was sitting in front of me, turn around and looked up at me with eyes that seemed to ask, "Are you following all of this?" I glanced around at the other jurors and saw many other puzzled expressions. Still, I continued writing as fast as I could on my yellow notepad.

According to the state prosecutor there were three main players in this trial: Darren Paulson, the defendant; Jared McDonald, the driver; and Bob Candlestick, the deceased. I drew a line between the names and put McDonald in the center because he was the person who knew both men prior to the night of the shooting. I also wrote down that pot may have been involved in past gatherings, and perhaps pot was the reason why McDonald wanted to introduce Paulson to Candlestick.

Prosecutor Albert continued. "Mr. McDonald called Mr. Paulson to make arrangements to meet. Usually, folks who are going to do those types of deals need to talk to each other face to face. Mr. McDonald, with Mr. Candlestick, drove over to where Mr. Paulson worked the third shift as a mechanic at a local trucking company. Mr. McDonald was in the driver's seat, and Mr. Candlestick was in the front passenger seat. Mr. McDonald backed into a parking space on the back row of the employee parking lot and called Mr. Paulson to inform him of their arrival. They waited for a moment, and then Mr. Paulson arrived, getting into the back seat, on the driver's side of the car.

"Mr. Candlestick and Mr. Paulson briefly exchanged greetings, and then they talked about the price of the marijuana. Evidently, the price was approximately $900 or $950 for a pound of marijuana. Mr. Candlestick got very upset about the price, turned around in his seat, and grabbed Mr. Paulson by the collar. There's not going to be a dispute that Mr. Candlestick turned around in his seat and reached back and grabbed Mr. Paulson by the collar.

"What Mr. McDonald, the only other living eyewitness, is going to say is that he heard Mr. Paulson say, 'You got it, you got it.' Now, it's not clear, and I don't believe the evidence will show it's clear, what was meant when he said 'You got it, you got it.' Nevertheless, we believe that Mr. McDonald will testify that Mr. Candlestick then calmed down and turned back around in his seat. Everything is over, it's done, and the disagreement is worked out.

"Apparently not, though, because the next thing Mr. McDonald would see happen was the dome light coming on in his car, and then he heard a loud explosion. Just one shot and then a few moments later, he heard two or three other shots. At that point, he put his head down and started his car. As he was driving away, he looked over at Mr. Candlestick, who was slumped over in his front seat.

"Mr. McDonald grabbed him by the head, and his head just flopped around. He knew he was still alive because he could hear him gurgling. He immediately took him to a medical center that was just a few minutes away. Mr. McDonald arrived at the emergency entrance and asked the medical staff on duty to help his friend, and then he went outside to wait in the parking lot in his car."

I was grateful that my pen did not run out of ink, because the prosecuting attorney was sharing a great deal of information that I wanted to write down. Sitting in my chair in the jury box, I felt I was getting a play-by-play account of the events that occurred that night. Still, it was hard to absorb it all, and I was not completely positive that I had a thorough understanding of everything that had happened.

I quickly reviewed my notes, which indicated that Paulson, the defendant, got into the rear seat on the driver's side of the car. Candlestick, the dead man, turned around in his front passenger seat and reached back to grab Paulson by the collar. There was a break in the heated exchange, then the dome light came on, and Paulson shot his gun as he was leaving the car. The bullet struck Candlestick, and the driver, McDonald, rushed him to a medical center that just happened to be a short distance from the trucking company's parking lot. I have included the following image to give you a better visual of the three main players as they were sitting in the parked car.

I didn't have much time to ponder my notes because the prosecuting attorney was about to conclude his opening statement. "At that time, the authorities had been notified, and you're going to hear from some of the responding officers later as witnesses," Albert told us. "You're going to hear from Officer Jason Roberts, who was one of the first police officers to arrive at the medical center. He's going to tell you that by the time they got there, they found out that Mr. Candlestick was deceased, and they learned that Mr. McDonald was still sitting in the parking lot at the medical center.

"Not knowing what was going on, other than that someone had been shot, Officer Roberts approached Mr. McDonald in his car. He had no idea if Mr. McDonald was the shooter or if he had a weapon. The officer will tell you that he yanked Mr. McDonald out of the car in what is called a felony takedown. He immediately put him in the back of his patrol car until he could determine what was going on.

"I anticipate Mr. Edwin, the defense attorney, is going to show you a diagram that shows the items discovered in the area of the scene.

You're going to hear that they located four of what they call 'cartridge cases,' commonly called shell cases. Those are the empty cartridges that bullets, when they're shot from a semi-automatic pistol, eject out of the gun.

Placement of main characters and some of the evidence submitted in the murder trial

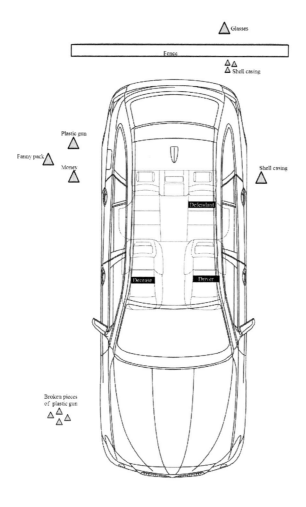

"You're going to hear that there were eyeglasses located there, glasses that one of the witnesses will testify are similar to the glasses worn by Mr. Paulson. You're also going to hear that there was a plastic gun located well behind where the vehicle was parked, with several small pieces of it found by the front wheel of where the vehicle would have been parked. You're going to be told that they found a blue fanny pack located at the rear of where the vehicle was parked. You're also going to hear that there were two wads of money found. Each wad contained a thousand dollars, and they were found lying on the pavement behind the vehicle, near where the shell casings were found, and near where the toy gun was found.

"Again, this is not going to be a whodunit type of trial. It's going to be a question of whether or not Mr. Paulson was justified in killing Mr. Candlestick. I'm going to ask you, ladies and gentlemen of the jury, not to make up your minds on this case until all the evidence is in, and you hear all the statements from the witnesses who are going to take the stand over the next few days.

"The State believes the evidence will show that Mr. Paulson was well out of the vehicle, well on his way from leaving the whole interaction with the people in the car. The evidence will show that everything was already done and over with when Mr. Paulson killed Mr. Candlestick. We will prove to you that this is not a case of self-defense; we will prove that this is a murder case. And when the State of Georgia rests its case, the State will be asking you to return a guilty verdict on all charges. Thank you."

While the District Attorney was speaking, I tried not to look at Paulson so that I would not jump to any conclusions based on his physical appearance. I also tried not to jump to any conclusions about the case based on my own history.

When I was 10 years old and my parents were divorcing, my father, who did not live with us, committed suicide. Three years later, my mom married again, and we moved into a trailer park. I was just 13, I felt my friends at school were treating me differently now, and I was having a hard time coping with the loss of my dad. Moving from a farmhouse that we had rented to a trailer park, I quickly became friends with some other 13-year-olds who were into drinking and smoking pot. These kids didn't care about my past; they just wanted another person to hang out with. Smoking pot, I found, was much easier than alcohol to conceal from others, including my mother and stepfather.

My oldest brother and my parents didn't really like the kids I was now calling my friends. I thought they were harmless and fun to be around, but most of all I felt accepted by them.

After a year and a half of living in the trailer park, a new family moved in. Although they seemed a little weird, I felt they were harmless. Jeff was a year younger than me, and his cousin Lori lived with them, too. Lori was a year older than me, and I thought she was the cutest girl to walk the earth. I started spending time with Jeff's family just so I could be in the same room with her.

One day, Jeff asked me to come over to his trailer home because his mom wanted to talk with me. She told me she desperately needed money, and she asked me to burn down their trailer home. In return, she would split the insurance money with me. Now, I had certainly done some unlawful things in the past 18 months since moving into the trailer park, but setting a trailer on fire was a huge deal. I told them I would have to think about it, and I left their trailer and never went back. I didn't know what to do, or who I should tell about the conversation, so I decided not to tell anyone.

A few weeks passed, and I went on a weekend trip with my mom and stepfather to my uncle's farm about three hours away. We came back that Sunday night to discover that two trailers had burned to the ground that weekend in our trailer park. One of the trailers was owned by the woman who had asked me to burn down her place so that she could collect the insurance money.

I took my bike and rode around the trailers, which were still smoldering a little. Jeff stopped me, and told me what had happened. Apparently, he had broken into the trailer next to his, stolen some items, and taken them back to his trailer. His mother found out, and she told him to burn down the trailer to get rid of his fingerprints. They started that fire and, since the trailer was right next to theirs, Jeff's mother decided to burn down her own trailer as well and collect the insurance money.

My first impression of them being harmless was definitely wrong. Jeff told me not to tell anyone about what they had done, and it took me two days before I finally told my oldest brother all I knew. He took me into the living room where I then told my mom. When the police came, I had to give a statement.

I remember feeling very sad for Jeff's family because I hadn't really wanted to hurt them. Life had been tough enough for them, and my confession had made it even more difficult. Jeff's mother eventually went to jail, and the children were taken into the state's custody. Despite my misgivings, though, I could not keep the truth to myself. I knew in my heart that I had done the right thing.

Now, I wondered if I might be sympathetic to one of the main characters in the trial since we potentially shared a similar past. My memory shifted back to what the defense attorney had asked me during the *voir dire* process. He had asked me, "Knowing yourself, is there any reason you can think of that would require Mr. Paulson to present evidence to prove his innocence? Knowing yourself, is there any reason that you could not wait until all the evidence is admitted and this Honorable Court presents the charges on the law before you make your decision about this case? Knowing yourself, do you believe you would have trouble keeping an open mind about this case until after you heard all the evidence? Knowing yourself, can you look at Mr. Paulson as being innocent until proven guilty?"

Suddenly, I began to question how well I really did know myself. How many more memories had I suppressed over the years? Would my past impact the way I saw the truth in the evidence that would come out in this case? Would I make up my own justifications, one way or the other, based on personal experiences? The excitement that I originally felt about being selected to this jury panel had evaporated, and now

I wondered whether I truly could be the fair, impartial, and unbiased juror that I had sworn under oath to be.

Edwin, the defense attorney, started his opening statement. "Today I'm going to share with you what happened on Wednesday, December 20th, of 2006, at approximately 8:45 in the evening. Mr. McDonald was driving a 1996 Chevy Caprice Classic with Mr. Candlestick in the front passenger seat. Mr. McDonald pulled into the Express Trucking Company's employee parking lot, planning to rob Mr. Paulson, my client. Mr. McDonald and Mr. Candlestick had a gun. It turned out to be a plastic gun with the red tip removed so no one would realize it was not a real Colt semi-automatic weapon."

This was new and interesting information to me. I was unaware that toy firearms were equipped with quarter-inch red or orange tips so they could be identified easily as fakes. In fact, I learned later that it is a federal offense to remove the orange tip, which helps law enforcement officers clearly differentiate real guns from toys. Edwin did not waste any time letting us know that McDonald and Candlestick had intended to rob his client.

"Bob Candlestick was wearing a dark hoodie, and a knit cap or skull cap that night. Jared McDonald backed his vehicle into the parking space. My client, Darren Paulson, was working the third shift from 6:30 p.m. to 3:30 a.m. as a mechanic fixing tractor trailers. He made about $42,000 to $44,000 a year at the trucking company.

"The events that night did not occur because of a drug deal gone bad as the prosecuting attorney told you. Mr. McDonald hardly knew anything about my client; they weren't close friends or buddies. Instead, Mr. McDonald's cousin was friends with my client.

"Anyhow, Mr. McDonald heard from his cousin that Darren was looking to buy a PlayStation 3, maybe two units if available. Darren had been taking care of his girlfriend's son, who was 8 years old in December of 2006. The child's name is Joshua, and Darren had been around him since he was 6 months old. You will learn that PlayStation 3s were just created by Sony around this time, and were priced at $600 in the stores. The demand was high for these new gaming devices, and the inventory levels were low.

"Mr. McDonald called Mr. Paulson the day before, Tuesday the 19th of December, 2006. He told Darren, 'I have three PlayStations for you. I know you're looking for them, and I'll sell them to you for $950 each. If you buy more than one, maybe I'll give you a discount. So bring money, and I'll come by your office tomorrow, and you can get your girlfriend's child a Christmas gift.'

"Mr. Paulson said, 'Great.'

"As Mr. McDonald was pulling into the parking lot with Mr. Candlestick in the vehicle, they called Mr. Paulson, 'Come on out. We're here with the PlayStations.' Darren explained, 'I'm working on a truck, so give me a few minutes.'

"Darren finished his work in his bay and went on his lunch break. On the way to meet Mr. McDonald, he went to his vehicle and retrieved $2,000. That was a lot of money to him, so Darren also placed his registered gun, which is a .380 caliber Bersa semi-automatic weapon, in his uniform-issued front jacket pocket.

"He did that because he had to walk through almost the entire employee parking to get to Mr. McDonald's car in the last row. It was late at night, it was dark, and so Darren put the $2,000 into his front-right pants pocket. He was simply hoping to get a PlayStation 3 as a Christmas present for his girlfriend's son Joshua."

At this point in his opening statements, I noticed that attorney Edwin was very detailed as he painted a picture of what he believed happened the night Candlestick lost his life. Calling his client by his first name, he pictured him as an honest, hardworking man, making above-average income for a person of his age. Edwin also made it clear the defendant was financially taking care of not only his girlfriend, but also her son.

Edwin's version of the reason for the meeting was quite a bit different from the version given by the prosecuting attorney. Edwin stated that the sole reason his client agreed to meet with McDonald was that he had a PlayStation 3 for sale. He described Paulson as desperately wanting to give Joshua a PlayStation 3 for Christmas, which was just five days away.

It was interesting the way attorney Edwin described Candlestick's clothing: a dark jacket was "a hoodie" and a hat was "a skull cap." It was a clever strategy because many people believe that robbers wear such clothing. As I mentioned in the beginning of Chapter One, I didn't realize how my personal beliefs structured the way I made critical decisions about my life and my reality. Obviously, the defense attorney was targeting some of the jurors' potential belief systems about how a robber might dress.

Edwin described that when his client approached the car from the front, he noticed someone was sitting in the front passenger seat. Paulson proceeded to open the rear passenger door, but Candlestick, whom he didn't expect to meet that night, had his seat pushed back and reclined. Paulson couldn't get his legs into the car, either, because the floorboard where the feet normally would rest was filled with items. McDonald said to Paulson, "Come around and get in behind me."

"Mr. Paulson proceeded around the rear of the car and got into the back seat behind Mr. McDonald as directed," defense attorney Edwin continued. "He shut the car door, and the dome light went off. Then Mr. Candlestick turned around over the seat and put his left hand on Darren's neck, grabbing him by the collar of his shirt and placing a gun in Darren's face. Mr. Paulson thought he was going to die.

"Mr. Candlestick shouted to Mr. Paulson, 'Give me, give it to me now. Give me the money, or I'm going to kill you.' Mr. Paulson saw his whole life pass before him. He made no sudden movements and instead put his hands up saying, 'You got it. You got it. Calm down.' He slowly put his hand into his right front pants pocket to retrieve the money.

"The gun was pointed at Mr. Paulson's forehead. Darren took out his wads of money and put them onto the seat next to him. Mr. Candlestick released his grip on Darren's neck and reached with his left hand to pick up the money. He then retreated to the front seat while keeping his gun pointed at Mr. Paulson.

"Mr. Paulson did not want to be in that car. He did not know when that car was going to pull away or if he would be alive when it did. He put his hand in his jacket pocket where his semi-automatic .380 caliber Bersa was. He put his other hand on the rear door handle and quickly opened the door. He took one step out and looked back. He saw Mr. Candlestick reaching for him. Mr. Paulson, expecting a barrage of bullets from Mr. Candlestick's gun hitting him, fired one time and continued to run away. Mr. Paulson fired only one time as he escaped the back seat of the car.

"When Mr. Paulson fled for his life from that car and jumped over the fence, he did not know that Mr. Candlestick was shot. He certainly did not know Mr. Candlestick was mortally wounded. Mr. Paulson was thinking that Mr. Candlestick and Mr. McDonald may have been coming after him, so Mr. Paulson hid in the woods behind his work place. He lost track of time. He lost the gun. He was not thinking straight because he was nervous and traumatized.

"Mr. Paulson then went back to his place of employment, but he did not want to stay there because he knew Mr. McDonald and Mr. Candlestick knew where he worked. He got in his car and pulled out of the parking lot, and he passed a Lawrenceville Police cruiser. Mr. Paulson did not stop; he did not stay. He wanted to get away from that area, so he left. He did not go home because he was afraid that Mr. McDonald and Mr. Candlestick might be waiting for him at his home. So he went to a friend's house, and found out a short time later that there was an arrest warrant out for him for murder.

"Mr. Paulson realized that Bob Candlestick had died, and he also realized that Mr. McDonald could not have told the truth to law enforcement. If Mr. McDonald had told the police that a gun had been placed in Darren Paulson's face, and that Mr. Paulson was a victim of an armed robbery, there would not be a warrant out for his arrest.

"Mr. Paulson spent the next six weeks at a friend's home in Gwinnett County. He didn't go to work, and he didn't go to the police. He didn't want to go see the police because he was afraid to meet with the Lawrenceville Police Department without an attorney, and he didn't think he could afford a lawyer.

"Later in the trial, you will hear that no evidence was found when the police searched Mr. Paulson's home. No marijuana was found, and no marijuana paraphernalia was found. You will learn that when Mr. Paulson was arrested, there was no marijuana present. There is no evidence of marijuana anywhere. The word 'marijuana' comes into play from Mr. McDonald because he came up with a story that would not get him into trouble, according to someone he spoke with from law enforcement.

"You will also learn that Mr. McDonald told law enforcement at the medical center that Mr. Candlestick had a gun pointed at my client. That statement will be denied by him, but you'll hear another witness from law enforcement contradict Mr. McDonald's denial. You will learn that Mr. McDonald is a convicted felon, and as a convicted felon, if he were to be involved in an armed robbery he would be in violation of his probation and could be sent to jail.

"During the trial you will also learn that Mr. McDonald told his uncle about his intentions to rob my client. Mr. McDonald told his uncle, Scott Target, that he was afraid that he was going to get arrested and charged with armed robbery because of the role he played that night.

"This is a tragic case. There is a loss of life, and that is serious. But Darren Paulson has asked you to take the oath, to be the jurors in this case. My client, Darren Paulson, has pleaded not guilty to the most serious crimes in the State of Georgia. Mr. Paulson is not guilty of murder, felony murder, aggravated assault, or the possession of a weapon during the commission of a crime. At the conclusion of this case, we will ask you to return those verdicts based upon the fact that Mr. Paulson was defending himself against an armed robbery and an aggravated assault. Thank you for your time."

I have heard the saying many times over the years that there are always two sides to every story, and I had just finished listening to two attorneys sharing two very different viewpoints on the same case. It was obvious that the whole truth and nothing but the complete truth would not be present in this trial.

Prosecutor Albert would have liked nothing better than to report back to his boss, the district attorney, that another bad guy was behind bars. Like the defense attorney, Albert often used very specific words to paint a picture in our minds – true or not – that the defendant shot Candlestick not out of self-defense, but out of revenge or anger.

The picture painted by Edwin, the defense attorney, was completely different. He, too, used specific words, sentences, and thoughts, although he did not necessarily claim they were true. Instead, he planted seeds of doubt in our minds, explaining that there were other possibilities about what had happened that night inside the car.

I understood now more than ever the importance of my role as a juror. I had taken an oath to interpret and filter what I saw and heard in court, and to focus on the truth to the best of my ability. Despite the conflicting reports, I felt confident that I could set aside my own past and look at Paulson as innocent until proven guilty.

Chapter Four

Seeking the Truth – Part One

After listening to the opening statements, I realized that the driver, the defendant, and the victim, if he were alive, would have had something in common – the desire that this tragic event had never occurred. All three men would have loved to have had a second chance to change their decisions and their behaviors so that their lives could have turned out drastically different.

The first witness was about to be called to the witness stand. I knew I must listen closely to the witnesses because they could possess personal motives that were much stronger than their desire to tell the truth, the whole truth, and nothing but the truth.

The first witness called to the stand by the prosecutor was Officer Jason Roberts. Prosecutor Albert said, "Raise your right hand. I swear by Almighty God that the evidence I shall give shall be the truth, the whole truth, and nothing but the truth."

Officer Roberts replied, "I do."

During the questioning, I learned that Roberts and another officer were working the DUI task force the night of the shooting. Their dispatcher re-routed them to the medical center emergency room with the only information known by police at the time – that a person had been shot. Upon arrival, Roberts spoke with the emergency room personnel, and they informed him that the subject, now in the trauma room, had been pronounced deceased.

The medical personnel also informed Roberts that a friend had dropped off the subject, and that the friend might still be in the parking lot. Roberts asked for a description, but all he was given was that the friend was a white male driving a white Chevy Caprice. Roberts immediately started searching the parking lot until he came upon a vehicle that matched the description given by the emergency room personnel.

As the policeman approached the car, he saw a white male slumped over in the driver's seat. At this time, the officer did not know if this was the shooter or if he was wounded, armed and dangerous, or under the influence of drugs. Roberts said he asked his partner to cover him and they both drew their weapons. Then Roberts verbally got the attention of the driver and ordered him out of the vehicle.

Once the officers could see both of the man's hands, "I basically reached in the car, grabbed him, pulled him out to the back of the car very quickly, and patted him down for weapons," Roberts said.

Prosecutor Albert asked, "What was the subject's demeanor at that point?"

Roberts replied, "He was very scared and very nervous. The subject was visibly shaking."

The policeman concluded his testimony with the prosecutor by describing that the only other involvement he had with the case was that he secured the subject by placing him in the back seat of his squad car until the lead investigator had arrived on the scene.

The cross-examination from defense attorney Edwin was brief. Edwin verified police procedures and steps that needed to be taken in any potential murder investigation. He also confirmed with the officer that it was important to secure the vehicle that the subject was driving to prevent contamination of such evidence as a shell casing, blood stains, or signs of a robbery.

Edwin asked the police officer, "Was Mr. McDonald evasive when you first met him and secured him in the back seat of your squad car?"

"Yes sir," Roberts replied. "The subject did not speak with me directly. He did speak with Detective Godskeep when he arrived a little later. The detective sat down in the back seat of the squad car, and they spoke there."

Edwin asked, "Can you tell the jury panel what you heard as Detective Godskeep spoke with Mr. McDonald while they were sitting in the back seat of your squad car?"

"They were not in the squad car for very long before the detective took the subject to his vehicle and transported him to the police station," Roberts said. "What I did hear was that he took his friend, the deceased, to meet with a white male, but he didn't give the name of this person. Mr. McDonald mentioned that the white man and the deceased had an argument.

"The next thing the subject heard was a gunshot followed by several other gunshots. Frankly, that is all I heard because two other detectives arrived and had the car impounded, and they took the subject to the police station for further questioning. At that point, I was released from the scene and went back to performing my duties on the DUI task force."

The next witness to take the stand was Jared McDonald, the driver of the car the night Bob Candlestick died. Again, prosecutor Albert said, "Raise your right hand. I swear by Almighty God that the evidence I shall give shall be the truth, the whole truth, and nothing but the truth."

McDonald replied, "I do."

During this questioning, I found myself having some difficulty understanding McDonald. He would attempt to answer a question, but more times than not he would end his answer with the question, "You know what I'm saying?" Obviously, McDonald possessed a very limited formal English vocabulary, although he certainly was well versed in street slang. As the testimony went on, prosecutor Albert deliberately slowed down his own speech to make his questions easier to understand.

McDonald confirmed that he was driving the car that night, and that he picked up Candlestick at a barbershop. He stated they both proceeded to meet with defendant Paulson at his place of work. Albert asked McDonald, "Was the deal to your knowledge going to go down at that meeting, or were they just making introductions before they consummated the deal?"

"They had never met or talked before," McDonald replied. "It could have been going down right there. I mean, but my main thing was I was just hooking them up with each other so I wouldn't have to be involved in it no more. You know what I'm saying?"

Albert asked, "What happened when Darren Paulson entered your car?"

"You know, he got in the car, and they both said, 'What's up?' You know, just acknowledging each other, I guess you'd say," McDonald said. "Then it was like something just clicked, and Bob turned around and, you know, he just grabbed Darren."

"So Bob Candlestick turned around and grabbed the defendant, Darren Paulson? Then what happened?"

McDonald replied, "You know, I asked him what he was doing. You know, he looked at me and told me to shut up. And I mean, it was like he let him go like as quick as he grabbed him, you know. I mean, you know what I'm saying? It was like he grabbed hold to him. I don't remember what Bob was saying to him, but I remember Darren saying something like, 'you got it, you got it,' and then Bob, just stopped. He just let him go."

Albert paused. "Okay, Bob Candlestick let Darren Paulson go, and then what happened?"

McDonald said, "Darren got out of the car. The dome light came on when the door opened … you know what I'm saying? He got out of the car, and that's when I heard the shot. Bob looked at me and told me to crank up the car. So I tried cranking up the car, you know what I'm saying? I mean Bob said, I don't know if he was talking to me or he was just saying, but he said, 'He shot me.' Then I drove pretty fast to the hospital, and they took Bob and put him in the wheelchair, and I never saw him alive again, you know what I'm saying?"

Continuing with this line of questioning, the prosecutor asked McDonald to review the chain of events that occurred upon his arrival at the emergency room. McDonald explained that he parked his car in the parking lot, and when he was asked why he stayed, he replied, "I don't know; I just moved the car. That's what I was thinking. You know what I'm saying?" The discussions continued, and McDonald denied throwing any evidence out of the car window prior to leaving the scene of the shooting and traveling to the medical center.

When McDonald was asked to describe his encounter with the police officer at the medical center parking lot, he said, "I can't really remember how they came up on me. I mean it wasn't nothing. Like they had no gun drawn on me or nothing like that. They weren't like rushing me."

Albert asked, "When the police arrived at your parked car, did you immediately tell them what happened when the first officers were there?"

"Not right off," McDonald said. "I was scared, and I've been taught not to trust the police. But eventually, you know, I told them that my friend got shot."

Albert did have McDonald verify that, at the time of this tragic event, defendant Paulson had facial hair, in contrast to his clean-shaven appearance in the courtroom that day. I found it interesting that both attorneys made a point to give the jury a visual about how the people appeared the evening of the shooting.

At the conclusion of McDonald's testimony to the prosecution, the judge released the jurors for lunch. We were escorted to the deliberation room for quite a while. Most of us just walked around, and a few of us took a restroom break. What I didn't know at the time was that the reason we had to wait in the deliberation room for so long was because the guards had to take McDonald to the cafeteria first. They didn't want the jury members bumping into him in the food line.

While we were waiting for the bailiff to come back and take us to lunch, some small talk broke out among the jury panel, and the youngest male juror started talking about the witness to whoever would listen. Soon one of the women joined in his conversation and said something about the way the witness was speaking. The next thing I heard was a deep conversation between the two of them about the witness, the attorney and, ultimately, the case.

One or two minutes into their conversation, I knocked on the conference room table quite hard with my knuckles. Everyone looked at me – some were quite startled – and I pointed out the window, saying how beautiful the day was outside. There was now a distinct silence in the room. I said, "I'm sorry that I interrupted your conversation, but the judge has made it very clear to us that we are not supposed to discuss the case among ourselves, or with anyone else for that matter, until we are told we can do so."

I received a few puzzled looks, and then some small talk resumed among the jurors, but it was not about the case. A few more minutes passed before the bailiff escorted us to the cafeteria.

After lunch, we were taken back to the courtroom, where defense attorney Edwin began his cross-examination of the driver of the car, Jared McDonald. Edwin asked McDonald to confirm that he had brought Candlestick to meet with Paulson for a marijuana transaction. Then Edwin asked if McDonald had any other evidence, besides his word, that he could share with the jury that would corroborate that this meeting was about marijuana. McDonald replied, "No sir."

The defense attorney then asked McDonald to confirm that he had an uncle named Scott Target, and that they had a close relationship. Once that was confirmed, Edwin said, "Earlier, you mentioned you 'were raised not to trust the police,' and my question to you now is: Is that what your uncle, Scott Target, taught you?"

McDonald enthusiastically replied, "No, sir."

Edwin continued his cross-examination with a series of questions regarding what McDonald said to the lead detective while he was still at the medical center parking lot. Obviously trying to determine the closeness of McDonald's relationship with the deceased, Edwin asked McDonald if he knew Candlestick's date of birth, his home address, his nickname, or his employment status. McDonald indicated to the jury panel that he didn't know the answers to those personal questions, and reaffirmed that he really didn't know the deceased very well because they had only met recently.

Edwin asked, "Did you not tell Detective Godskeep while at the medical center parking lot, sitting in the back of the police car, that Mr. Candlestick pulled out a plastic air gun and pointed it at Mr. Paulson. Do you remember saying that?"

McDonald replied, "No sir, I did not."

Quickly, Edwin asked, "Now, you're not telling this jury that Mr. Candlestick did not have a gun, are you?"

McDonald said, "No, I mean I'm not saying that he did. I'm not saying that he didn't. You know what I'm saying? I mean, you know it ain't like I searched him before he got in my car. Do you know what I'm saying?"

Increasing the pace of his line of questioning, Edwin asked, "No, I actually don't know what you're saying. But, let me ask you about when you testified previously in a proceeding in April of 2008. Do you remember that testimony?"

This is the first I had heard about a previous proceeding. I looked around at my fellow juror members, and they, too, were glancing around in puzzlement. I quickly wrote down that there apparently had been a previous trial and then turned my attention back to the defense attorney.

McDonald replied, "Yes sir."

Edwin asked, "You testified then that you were not sure whether Mr. Candlestick had a gun or didn't have a gun, right?"

McDonald said, "Yes sir."

Picking up the pace in an obvious attempt to get the witness to falter, Edwin shouted, "What are you trying to tell this jury here today?

Did Mr. Candlestick have a gun or not? You were only 2 or 3 feet away from him in the front seat. What's your answer today?"

McDonald paused as if searching his mind for the right answer and then replied, "I'm not, I mean. I don't know if he had a gun or not at the time. You know what I'm saying? I honestly don't know."

Continuing in a loud voice, Edwin asked, "Did you not tell your uncle, Scott Target, that you, on the way to the hospital after the shooting, threw the gun out of your car because you wanted to hide the evidence? You knew as a convicted felon that if you were part of an armed robbery you could go to jail, isn't that true?"

McDonald began looking around the room as if seeking someone to help him. Finally, he replied, "Yes."

Before McDonald had a chance to say another word, Edwin said, "Yes, you threw the gun out the window?"

McDonald replied, "No! I mean, yes. I mean, I knew I was still on probation, and I could get into trouble. No, I didn't, you know what I'm saying? No, I didn't throw a gun out the window."

Edwin continued, "Then why would your uncle tell a private investigator that you advised him in March 2007 that you threw what's now State's Exhibit Number 25, the plastic gun, out your window on the way to the medical center?"

McDonald replied, "I don't know why. No sir."

For several minutes during this series of questions it looked as if the defense attorney had the driver of the car frazzled – perhaps enough that he might commit perjury or incriminate himself. When that didn't happen, Edwin paused, looked at his notes, and proceeded to focus on a different line of questioning. He got McDonald to confirm that Candlestick moved violently toward Paulson, who was sitting in the back seat behind the driver. McDonald also confirmed with the defense attorney that he heard Paulson say, "You got it, you got it."

Then Edwin asked McDonald, "Did you hear Mr. Candlestick say 'I'm going to kill you? Give me your money, or I'm going to kill you?'"

McDonald replied, "No. I don't remember. I'm not going to sit here and tell you something, and it not be true. I don't remember what was said, you know what I'm saying? I don't remember."

As Edwin concluded his cross-examination, Jared McDonald confirmed that he was never charged with a crime in this case and had never spent any time in jail for his involvement in it. McDonald could not explain how the $2,000 found on the ground where he parked his car that night got there, nor could he explain who the plastic gun belonged to, or why it was found in the same area in which the car was parked. McDonald did confirm that the electric windows in his car were fully functional the evening of the shooting.

After McDonald's testimony, the judge called for a 15-minute restroom break. During our recess, I remember looking at the other jury members in amazement. I had just witnessed the defense attorney, through his rapid-fire questioning, have McDonald seemingly up against the ropes. I was truly waiting for that Mike Tyson-type knock-out question and then an answer from McDonald that would shed the light of truth on what transpired in the car that tragic night. But that moment never occurred, and the witness was released by the judge.

As we were walking back into the courtroom, I was trying to wrap my head around what defense attorney Edwin had said about a previous trial, and why we were not told about that before the case was begun.

The next witness to take the stand and take the oath was Officer Alicia Zillow, who had collected the evidence found in the parking lot where the shooting took place. Officer Zillow had 26 years of experience in law enforcement, much of which was spent with the crime scene investigation unit. She also had attended numerous crime scene courses and had obtained several certifications through the Georgia Division of International Association for Identification. She was considered by both attorneys to be an expert in collecting evidence.

Through the dialogue with the prosecuting attorney, I learned that when Zillow arrived on the crime scene, the Gwinnett County Crime Scene Investigative Unit was already there. She did an initial walk-through upon her arrival, explaining how careful she was not to disturb anything that might have been lying on the ground. She mentioned that her primary role was to help collect any evidence that was discovered.

Zillow conveyed the standard investigative procedures by letting the jury know that when items of interest are identified as out of place at a crime scene, notes are made about them. "When all the potential evidence has been collected and noted, then we hand over all our findings to the lead investigator, and he determines how to use our findings during his investigation of the crime," she explained.

I have to admit that beyond learning how the investigative unit actually handles crime scenes, the submitting of the physical evidence was the most tedious part of the trial. One item at a time, all pieces of evidence were tagged with identification numbers and verified by Zillow as to their legitimacy according to her initial official report. Once she verified an item as physical evidence or a photograph of the evidence found at the scene, it was formally published in open court.

After the items or photographs were published in court by the judge, the attorneys asked Zillow to explain to the jury what the evidence was and how it was found to be positioned at the crime scene. A projector and a large screen on the wall were used to show us photographs detailing the inside of the car where Candlestick was shot.

Aerial photographs of the scene helped us visualize the movements of the car as well as the defendant as he left the vehicle. One particular photograph of the deceased lying on a metal table, his eyes wide open, hit me pretty hard. Seeing that photograph made me remember again just why I was in this courtroom listening to this case. Someone died as a result of a gunshot. I, along with 11 other people had been called upon to listen to and view the evidence, and ultimately determine if any Georgia laws had been broken.

After all the evidence was submitted, defense attorney Edwin focused his questions to Zillow on potential fingerprints found on the various items of evidence that were published. Through his line of questioning, I learned that fingerprints can be successfully retrieved from money, from a plastic gun, and from the material from which a fanny pack is constructed. I also learned that if the evidence is mishandled or contaminated before the scene has been secured, then the credibility of a piece of evidence could be destroyed.

The judge released the witness and told the jury that we were in recess until the next morning. I was emotionally drained. Driving home, I started to reflect and sort out the information I had heard from the attorneys and the witnesses. I felt sad because I could still mentally see the picture of Candlestick's lifeless body on that metal table. I was confused about a previous trial that was mentioned and why the jury was not given any information about that trial. Many times throughout the day I had wanted to raise my hand and be called upon by the judge so that I could ask questions directly to the witnesses and the attorneys.

Arriving home, I was greeted by my two happy dogs, who wagged their tails in feverish glee. I could smell dinner cooking, and knew Lynda was at work in the kitchen. Although saddened by the court case, at the same time I felt blessed for what God had granted me.

Chapter Five

Seeking the Truth – Part Two

I woke up Wednesday morning eager to hear testimony from more witnesses. The next witness to take the stand was Raoul Ford, an employee of the trucking company where Darren Paulson worked. Ford had just happened to park his car in the same parking space where Candlestick was shot. The only reason Ford took the witness stand was that when he stepped out of his car that night, he literally stepped on $2,000 in U.S. currency. Ford testified under oath that he thought it was his lucky day, but decided to take the money into the trucking company office and inquire if anybody had reported losing any money. Just as Ford was talking to the dispatcher, a police car with lights flashing stopped in front of the office door. Ford greeted the officer and told him about stepping on the money. The officer confiscated the wads of cash, and that was the extent of Ford's involvement in this case. I am sure Ford had some mixed emotions about finding the money and then quickly having to give it up.

The next witness to take the stand was Raymond Hunter, a lead mechanic at the trucking company where Darren Paulson had worked. On the stand for less than five minutes, Hunter explained that Paulson had told him he was taking a lunch break. He said he had seen Paulson in the parking lot around the time of the shooting.

The lead detective was the next witness called by the prosecutor. After being sworn in, Jon Godskeep told us he had been a police officer for 25 years and a detective for 11. On call the weekend of the shooting, he was notified by dispatch that he was to drive immediately to the medical center and call his lieutenant for further instructions. Godskeep was told by the lieutenant that the man who brought the victim to the medical center was still in the parking lot, and that he should talk with him.

The detective went into the emergency room and was directed to the deceased by Sgt. Kenny Boone. Once Godskeep had a visual of the deceased, he was directed by Boone to the front parking lot and the patrol car, where McDonald was sitting in the back seat. The door was propped open, and McDonald's legs were sprawled outside.

The detective told us that he first confirmed that McDonald was the person who had brought the deceased to the medical center. Godskeep could tell McDonald was nervous, scared, and terribly upset; in fact, he told us that he could see the Caprice driver visibly shaking as he sat down beside him in the police cruiser.

Albert asked the detective, "Would you please tell the jury how you proceeded with your investigation with Mr. McDonald?"

Godskeep replied, "Mr. McDonald said he picked up the deceased at some location that I do not recall at the moment. Once Mr. Candlestick was in the car with Mr. McDonald, they proceeded to the Express Trucking Company, where they were to meet with an acquaintance of Mr. McDonald's. A phone call was made to the defendant, Mr. Paulson, and they waited in the car until he arrived. When Mr. Paulson showed up a few minutes later, he got in the seat behind Mr. McDonald, Mr. McDonald introduced the two of them, and Mr. Paulson and Mr. Candlestick then began a conversation about a transaction."

Albert asked, "Did he tell you what the transaction was at that time?"

Godskeep replied, "He said it was a marijuana transaction. He then said there was some conversation, a price was given to Mr. Candlestick, and a verbal altercation started. He mentioned he thought Mr. Candlestick thought the price was too expensive. Then he said at one point that Mr. Candlestick, who was sitting in the front passenger seat, turned around and grabbed Mr. Paulson by the shirt with both hands. Mr. McDonald said he heard Mr. Paulson say, 'Okay, okay, you got it, you got it.' Mr. McDonald said after he heard those words from Mr. Paulson, Mr. Candlestick turned back around and sat back in his seat.

"Mr. McDonald said as soon as Mr. Candlestick turned around, he felt a weight shift in the car as if someone was getting in or out. Then the dome light came on, and he heard a loud explosion from behind him. He said he grabbed his head and tried to get as close to the floor as he possibly could. Mr. McDonald mentioned he might have heard another shot or two, but he was not clear about that. He said he then started the car and drove away as fast as he could. He got out of the parking lot where Mr. Paulson worked and looked over at Mr. Candlestick and heard some type of gurgling noise. It looked as if Mr. Candlestick was unconscious, leaning against the passenger door. The medical center was about one mile away, and that is where he stopped to get help for Mr. Candlestick.

"He said he ran into the emergency room and said, 'Someone's been shot.' And there were people who came out and assisted him. Mr. Candlestick was a big guy, 220 pounds and a little over 6 feet tall."

As I sat in the jury box, I had listened to the prosecuting and defense attorneys in their opening statements tell us a little about what happened that night. I had listened to the driver of the car as he sat in the witness stand telling the jury his version of what he recalled happening the night Candlestick lost his life. Now, I had just heard the lead detective, Jon Godskeep, tell the jury what he remembered that McDonald told him about what happened that night. I was trying very hard to keep the notes on my yellow pad sectioned off so that I would know which witness said what as they were describing the chain of events that night. I was quite concerned that the important little details that were different from each witness would ultimately be blurred together as I sought the truth.

Albert said, "Thank you for outlining for us what Mr. McDonald told you about what happened that tragic night. Now, if you would, please tell us about your interaction with the medical investigator from the medical examiner's office."

Godskeep responded, "The medical investigator shows up at the scene when there has been a homicide, which is a death other than natural circumstances. It is his job to go out and assess the scene, and speak to the officers involved in the case. When he completes the initial interview, he then sends the report to the medical examiner assigned to the case.

"In this case, Lyle Mielke was assigned to this investigation, and I explained to him what I have basically told the jury here today. I also explained to Investigator Mielke that I had not been at the location of the shooting, and if he needed to speak with someone there, he could contact my lieutenant to get his input."

Albert asked, "During your discussion with Investigator Mielke, did you recall telling him that McDonald provided you with Candlestick's name, address, and date of birth?"

I thought to myself, what was the significance of this question?

Godskeep mulled the question for a moment. "It has been over four years ago, but I do not recall Mr. McDonald knowing that information to share with me," he said finally.

"Do you remember telling Investigator Mielke that the deceased had in his possession a handgun?" Albert continued. My eyes were laser focused on the lead investigator, and my ears were highly tuned with anticipation. I knew the answer that was going to be given at this very moment could impact my view of this case and perhaps allow a revelation in my efforts for seeking the truth.

Godskeep replied in one word, "No."

I looked around at the other jury members, and a few of them looked back toward me for a second or two before we turned back to hear the conclusion of the exchange of information between Albert and Godskeep. I learned that McDonald gave a physical description of Paulson to the lead investigator, and then a warrant for felony murder was issued. Later, the lead investigator obtained a photo of Paulson and reached out to the media, which put his name and picture on the news. Godskeep also contacted the U.S. Marshal Service and asked for its help in tracking down Paulson. The U.S. Marshal Service was successful in finding Paulson about six weeks after the night of the shooting. We were told he had been staying with a friend nearby.

The defense attorney's cross-examination had a completely different tone; Edwin immediately began questioning the integrity of the investigation under Godskeep's supervision. Edwin expressed his concern that the lead investigator did not take the time and energy to go to the location where the shooting took place. His point to the jury was that as the lead investigator, Godskeep should have visited the location where most of the physical evidence was gathered.

Edwin continued to attempt to place a dark cloud over the head of the lead investigator by giving the jury a brief job description of his position. I learned that the lead investigator receives all reports that are written by fellow law enforcement officers involved with the case. He or she is given all forensic data collected to ascertain what may have occurred at the crime scene, and the lead investigator has the ability to order additional scientific tests from the Georgia Bureau of Investigation laboratories. Finally, the lead investigator is responsible for assembling all of that information into a single report.

Although no reply from the lead investigator would have satisfied the defense attorney, Edwin asked why Godskeep did not order fingerprint tests. More specifically, he asked why he didn't demand fingerprint tests to be conducted for the money, the fanny pack, and the plastic gun that was found in the parking space where McDonald parked his vehicle. The self-assured Godskeep indicated that he thought the parking lot was a high traffic area and most likely the evidence would have been contaminated by other people touching the items.

I continued to listen to the defense attorney question the decisions made by the lead investigator. Godskeep confirmed that many pieces to the puzzle – the details of what happened the night Candlestick died – were provided by McDonald, a convicted felon. The lead investigator agreed when Edwin suggested that sometimes witnesses can concoct a story because they have their own agendas, such as avoiding arrest.

Defense attorney Edwin obviously was concerned that Godskeep was using the information given by McDonald as fact, and then basing evidentiary decisions about the case on them. And if that information was wrong, intentionally or not, then there could be a major issue with the integrity of the evidence in the case.

In a stern tone, the defense attorney told us that he was going to skip over the lead investigator's testimony on what he stated to be the truth regarding his conversation with the medical investigator that night at the medical center. Edwin said he would address those specific comments by bringing the medical investigator to the witness stand a little later in the trial. My interest was piqued as I wondered why he was going to wait.

I also wondered if the investigation by Godskeep was the best it could have been. The lead investigator had stated earlier that he had been on call the night the dispatcher phoned him – at about 9:30 p.m. What had the lead investigator been doing on his off time that night? Was he watching a movie and enjoying some popcorn with his family, or was he consuming a few beers while playing pool with some buddies?

Neither attorney asked what the lead detective was doing the night he received the call to go to work – even though his actions earlier in the evening could have impacted the conversation he had with McDonald. How vested was Godskeep in thoroughly examining Candlestick's death? I am confident the prosecuting attorney would not have appreciated my speculation.

Edwin concluded his cross-examination by confirming with Godskeep that his investigation did not turn up any evidence of marijuana, either in the vehicle or at Paulson's home when searched. The defense attorney also asked Godskeep if he had any evidence that would indicate who would have been the buyer or the seller of the potential marijuana transaction. The lead investigator said he could not prove who the potential buyer or seller was, or who truly owned the money that was found that night. Godskeep confirmed that he obtained the answers to all of those questions from McDonald, the driver of the car.

After lunch, we returned to the jury assembly room. There, I was approached by one of the women on the jury panel, who asked if she could tell me something. I said that if her question was not directly about the case, she was more than welcome to tell me anything. At the time, I did not even know her name.

The woman introduced herself as Rosemary, and told me she and two other women had appreciated how I had rapped my knuckles on the table in the deliberation room to remind the group about not discussing the case, as the judge had ordered. Those three women wanted me to be the foreman of the jury panel.

Rosemary also said she faced a dilemma. She was sitting next to a juror named Sam in the jury box, and he often made noises when a witness answered a question or when the attorneys asked questions. These grunts and mumbling noises sometimes were sounds of approval, and sometimes sounds of disgust. Sam was unintentionally influencing this juror, as well as distracting her. Rosemary asked me what I could do about the situation.

I suggested that we remind the whole group not to discuss the case or let their body language or verbal expressions indicate they were in favor of or against any thoughts a witness or attorney might share. I told her we could ask Adams, the bailiff, to have that conversation with the group. At that exact moment, the bailiff came into the assembly room, and I reviewed with him the scenario just discussed with Rosemary. He agreed to make the announcement as soon as he took us from the holding room to the jury deliberation room.

When the 12 of us got back to the deliberation room, Adams told the group that we should not discuss the case or give off any expressions one way or another while sitting in the jury box. Adams then left the room, only to return a few minutes later and ask me to go with him. It turned out that Adams had told the judge what had happened, and now the judge wanted to speak with me.

I sat down in the first seat in the jury box with the judge, both attorneys and Paulson present. The judge began asking me questions about Sam, but I explained that I did not actually witness him making the noises or physically making gestures. The only reason I was aware of them was because one of the jury members, Rosemary, told me that Sam was distracting her and some others in the jury box.

The judge thanked me and told me to return to the deliberation room. In less than a minute Adams was back, now asking Rosemary to follow him. Everyone seemed curious about why we were called out of the room, but no one asked me what was happening.

Rosemary came back after about three minutes, and Adams then asked Sam to come with him. So now, Sam was the third person called out in less than 10 minutes. When Sam arrived back in the jury room a few minutes later, we were all asked to return to the jury box. I remember thinking, as we were walking back to the courtroom, that there was enough drama with the trial itself; we jurors did not need to add any more to our day. Once we took our seats, the trial continued right where it had left off.

Chapter Six

Seeking the Truth – Part Three

The next witness to take the oath was the medical examiner. Dr. Patti Filzen was considered by the court to be an expert witness in the field of forensic pathology, largely because she had performed nearly 2,000 autopsies and external exams. Filzen also had supervised nearly 800 exams done by residents and fellows in their training programs, and she had testified as an expert witness in the State of Georgia more than a hundred times.

Filzen confirmed that she performed the internal exam portion of Candlestick's autopsy. She testified that the bullet entered the left hand wrist and exited through the other side of the wrist. The bullet then traveled into his left chest, passed through his ribs and damaged his left lung. The bullet also passed through three very large blood vessels at the top of the heart, allowing blood to escape into Candlestick's chest cavity. Finally, the bullet entered the right chest cavity, damaging the right lung and stopping just beneath the skin of the right side of his chest.

Filzen stated that the legal term of the cause of death was homicide. When asked by the prosecuting attorney if that was the same as murder, she replied, "No. Homicide is not necessarily the same as murder. Murder would be a type of crime that somebody might be charged with.

Homicide is just a category that is based on the circumstances that we use for vital statistic purposes. To a medical examiner, a homicide indicates that the death was the result of another's actions or death caused by another person."

During the cross-examination, the defense attorney had Filzen confirm that the type of wound that Candlestick received would not kill him instantly. Filzen also confirmed that in the first several minutes after Candlestick sustained the gunshot wound to the chest, it would be possible for him to talk and even walk. "Eventually, the gravity of the injury would take over and eliminate those basic functions from occurring again," she said.

Edwin then turned the focus of his questions to Candlestick's physical position in the front seat, compared to Paulson's in the back seat. The defense attorney asked Filzen to help the jury understand the bullet's pathway by drawing a line that connected the entrance and exit wounds from the wrist to the entrance wound in the left side of his chest.

"If Mr. Candlestick was shot while sitting in the front passenger seat of a sedan with his left hand extended out, and the shooter is standing in the rear driver's side open-door area, would there be anything inconsistent with the bullet's pathway?" he asked, and Filzen replied, "No."

Edwin then asked, "Again, regarding the pathway of the bullet wound, would it be possible for the bullet pathway to exist as it did if Mr. Candlestick was turned away from the shooter?"

Filzen replied, "No, because that would not line up with the entrance and the exit wound of the wrist and the chest."

The defense attorney concluded his cross-examination by having Filzen confirm that there was nothing that would have prevented Candlestick from holding a gun in his right hand at the precise time the bullet entered his left wrist and chest. Edwin also had Filzen confirm that because gunpowder or stippling was not present on Candlestick's wrists or chest; the shooter had to be at least 3 feet away. Edwin looked at the jury and said, "At least 3 feet away would place Paulson somewhere outside the vehicle when he pulled the trigger, and that is the reason no shell casing was found inside the car."

Edwin created a makeshift seating arrangement using chairs from the courtroom. He acted as if he were the passenger, reaching behind to grab Paulson in the back seat and showing the jury the potential movement of Candlestick in relationship to the path of the bullet. It was a powerful visual for me. I concluded that there was only one possible angle for the bullet to have entered in Candlestick's left wrist.

After a 15-minute recess, the defense attorney called his first witness, Lyle Mielke, the forensic medical investigator for the medical examiner's office who performed the Candlestick autopsy. The medical investigator indicated that he was called to the medical center to examine a 26-year-old, black male who had been shot dead. Mielke arrived at the emergency room around 11:30 p.m. to gather additional information, examine the deceased, and arrange for transport to the county morgue. His job was to assist the medical examiner in the case by conducting a preliminary investigation into Candlestick's death. He took notes and filed them with his findings in a report that was sent to the medical examiner's office.

The purpose of this process is to provide Filzen with some sort of background information on what the deceased might have been involved in before the medical examination took place. The medical investigator made it clear that the report he filed had nothing to do with the criminal investigation being worked by other officers.

Edwin approached Mielke with the court's permission and handed him a copy of the report he had filed, based on discussions with the lead investigator. Mielke confirmed that the document was his report and his findings. The defense attorney acknowledged that he understood that at the time Mielke arrived at the medical center, a live criminal investigation was taking place. Information was being updated and made available to the officers from multiple locations that evening. Edwin said, "I want to ask you, did Detective Godskeep tell you that his preliminary investigation indicated that, while negotiating a price for drugs, Candlestick and the seller began to argue and curse at one another?"

Mielke replied, "Yes, he did."

Edwin continued, "Did Detective Godskeep tell you that Mr. Candlestick pulled out a plastic air gun and pointed it at the seller? Please sir, review your notes if necessary."

Mielke replied, "Yes, he did."

Edwin then asked, "Did Detective Godskeep tell you that the seller got out of the car and pulled a handgun from his clothing and shot Mr. Candlestick?"

Again, Mielke replied, "Yes, he did."

I was stunned to hear this major contradiction in statements. Earlier, Detective Godskeep had told the prosecuting attorney that he had not told Mielke that Candlestick was in possession of a gun, even if later it proved to be a toy. Now I completely understood why Edwin said he would wait to address the claims from the detective regarding what he told the medical investigator during the opening hours of his investigation. I was not sure how I was going to use this information as I wrote down everything on my yellow legal pad as fast as I could.

Edwin had the medical investigator confirm that Godskeep told him that the driver thought there was one shot in the car and another shot fired at the car as it drove away. The medical investigator also confirmed that Godskeep said the driver of the vehicle identified the deceased's name, address, and date of birth and further explained that notification of death of the next-of-kin had been made to Candlestick's father by representatives of the police department.

Edwin concluded his examination by asking, "And you got all of that information that you just told the ladies and gentlemen of the jury from whom?"

Mielke replied, "From Detective Godskeep."

As the prosecutor stood to cross-examine the medical examiner, I wondered what possible questions he could ask him that could reverse what I had just heard. I was seeking the truth, and I knew I would have to decide at some point in the near future who was speaking the truth, the whole truth, and nothing but the truth.

During his cross-examination, Albert painted a picture for the jury of what was happening real time in the medical center as Mielke conducted his investigation. Mielke's discussions with Godskeep and potentially another officer or two took place in a busy emergency room, where patients were receiving critical care and being rolled into different rooms. Phones were ringing, and the ceiling speakers were constantly calling doctors and nurses to various rooms.

In other words, Albert explained, these discussions – where preliminary findings were reviewed – did not take place in a peaceful and quiet executive conference room; they were in an area that was buzzing, to say the least. The men, squashed against a wall to stay out of the way, had their notepads out and were scribbling in the margins of their official forms. In addition, the detective was receiving calls on his cell phone, and the radio on the police officer's left shoulder was receiving real-time updates on the investigation.

Albert asked the medical examiner, "Were you scribbling notes on a sheet of paper and you later typed those notes or perhaps had someone type those notes into a report for you? Do you have the scribbled notes with you here today?"

Mielke responded, "Yes, my notes would have probably been recorded on the rear or the margin of one of our death reports, which are about 5 inches wide and 6 inches long. I believe the actual notes were discarded when the final report was typed and submitted to the medical examiner's office."

Albert concluded his cross-examination by asking the medical examiner, "Is it possible that you could have overheard some bits of information from the police officers' radio or directly from the cell phone the detective was using and wrote that information down, and that information from other sources was actually attributed to Detective Godskeep in your note-taking?"

Mielke looked at Albert, cocking his head a little to one side as he replied, "If you are asking me is it possible that could have happened as you just outlined, I would have to say yes, it is a possibility."

The defense attorney chose not to do a redirect and left that answer to be the final words we heard from the medical investigator.

It had been helpful for the prosecutor to give us a graphic description about how the scene inside the emergency room area may have been that night as the police and medical department conducted their investigations. This particular witness seemed to me to have nothing to gain or lose by sharing his notes with the jury. He was not part of this case, trying to prove one thing or another. Instead, he was simply telling us the contents of the report he had filed over four years ago.

The defense attorney called his second witness, Paulson. Like all the other witnesses, the defendant took the oath to tell the truth, the whole truth, and nothing but the truth.

From the beginning of this direct examination, the defense attorney, through his questioning of the defendant, attempted to present his client as a decent citizen who had a solid, good-paying job, and who had just purchased a home. They discussed his girlfriend's son, Joshua, and how Paulson was helping to care for them both. Paulson confirmed to us that he was looking to obtain a PlayStation 3 for Joshua because it was only a few days before Christmas, and that is how he got caught in a bad situation, courtesy of McDonald and Candlestick.

Listening to Paulson's testimony, I decided it was possible that Paulson's desire to purchase a PlayStation 3 for Joshua could have led him to meet with McDonald at 9:30 that night in a dark parking lot. Still, I wondered what the probability was that the meeting actually was about a PlayStation 3.

The bottom line, though: It didn't matter what the meeting was for. I quickly started to refocus on the defendant sitting in the witness stand because I didn't want to miss a single word that was said.

Paulson declared that he was actually friends with McDonald's older cousin, Don Duffey. The two had been roommates, but at the time of the shooting, Duffey was incarcerated for a reason not mentioned. Mc-

Donald had his cousin's cell phone with Paulson's contact information stored in it. According to Paulson, about one week before the shooting, McDonald called Paulson on that cell phone, indicating he was down on his luck and needed some gas money to get back home. They made arrangements on the cell phone to meet at the guard shack where Paulson worked, and Paulson gave McDonald $50 for gas money. Paulson indicated that after giving McDonald the $50, he didn't think he would hear from him again.

Five days later, Paulson stated, he received another call from McDonald, this one claiming he had acquired three PlayStations and wanted to know if Paulson wanted to buy one or two of them. Excited to get a Christmas present for Joshua, Paulson agreed, and they made plans to meet in the parking lot where Paulson worked. When McDonald arrived as planned, he called Paulson, who then went to his own car to retrieve the $2,000 and his registered .380 caliber Bersa handgun. He mentioned that it was a dark parking lot, and he was carrying $2,000 cash in his pants pocket, so he put his handgun in the front pocket of his work-issued uniform coat.

The defense attorney asked Paulson to describe what happened when he approached the car that night. Paulson said he walked up to the car and was surprised to see that someone was in the passenger seat. Not expecting another person to be present, he opened the back door behind the passenger's seat and attempted to get in. However, Paulson said, the passenger had his seat reclined all the way back and there were many items on the floor board where passengers would normally put their feet.

The defendant said he then walked behind the car and sat in the rear seat behind the driver, McDonald. He continued with his testimony by saying that as soon as he shut the door, Candlestick turned around, grabbed him by the collar, pulled him toward him, and put a gun right in front of his forehead. Candlestick then yelled, "Give me your money, or I'll kill you."

The defense attorney asked, "Mr. Paulson, how did you feel at this very moment?"

The defendant replied, "I thought if I didn't cooperate, he would kill me. I felt like he was going to kill me." Paulson then stated that he was afraid, so he put up both of his hands in surrender. With the gun still pointed at his forehead, he very slowly reached down with his right hand into the pocket where he had placed the money, and he put the $2,000 on the seat next to him. When Candlestick reached for the money lying on the seat, he released his grip around Paulson's neck with his left hand, and Candlestick shifted his body to get the money and put it in the front seat with him.

Paulson furthered testified, "When Mr. Candlestick took the money he started to turn back around in his seat, and that is when he took his eyes off of me. He still had his gun pointed at me, but when he turned around, I put my hand on my gun and reached with my other hand for the back door handle. When the door opened, the dome light came on. Mr. Candlestick reached out to grab me with his left hand, and that is when, while I was exiting the car, I shot my weapon one time to save my life."

Paulson mentioned that he did not turn back and shoot anymore at the car or anyone in it. As a reminder, investigators found no bullet holes inside or outside the car. Paulson informed us that he ran up and over the fence directly behind the car, fell onto his back, and his glasses fell off his face. He said it was possible his gun accidentally went off three times as he climbed the fence, which is why shell casings were found there. Then he ran into the nearby woods, where he hid for an undisclosed amount of time.

At this point in the defendant's testimony, the defense attorney asked the judge for permission for Paulson to leave the witness stand. The defense attorney requested that they perform role play to give the jury a better visual on how the events in the car played out according to the defendant. The judge granted this request over the objection of the prosecutor.

Edwin used three chairs: one for the driver, one for the passenger and one positioned in the back of the driver's chair. He played the part of the passenger, Candlestick, and Paulson played the role of himself in the back seat. In slow motion, Edwin reached behind him and grabbed

Paulson by the shirt. Using the plastic gun already submitted as evidence, he pointed the gun at Paulson's forehead. Edwin continued his role play by verbally demanding that Paulson give him the money, or he would kill him.

Paulson put his hands up and said, "Okay, okay, you got it." He then reached into his pocket, pulled out the imaginary $2,000 and placed the money next to him. As he turned and reached for the imaginary money, Edwin took his eyes off Paulson, who immediately reached for the imaginary car door and his imaginary pistol. He stepped out of his seat, pointed the imaginary gun and pulled the trigger as he walked away from the chairs lined up in the courtroom. It was a powerful illustration, and it did give me a better visual explanation on how it was physically possible for the events of that night to have happened just as Paulson had testified.

During the cross-examination by the prosecutor, Albert had Paulson confirm that since 2008, the year of the previous trial, the defendant had in his possession the entire State of Georgia's file on the case. And having access to the complete file had given him ample time to prepare his statements for the jury while he was on the witness stand, Albert said. The prosecutor also pointed out that Paulson had the privilege of sitting through the entire trial and hearing all of the witnesses, while the other witnesses during this trial had been sequestered.

Albert mentioned that he understood Paulson worked the night shift, but he wondered out loud why, if Paulson cared so much for Joshua, he didn't take some time during the day to meet McDonald – even if that meant that he would not get as much sleep before heading to work.

If the three of them had met during the day, Albert continued, Paulson might not have had to walk around with $2,000 in his pocket at night, and he would not have had to bring his handgun to protect himself while he was walking to the car for the so-called PlayStation 3 exchange. Albert asked Paulson, "Why didn't you meet Mr. McDonald at the guard shack like you did previously when you gave him $50 for gas money?"

Paulson replied, "The price was something that we were going to negotiate. He said he had more than one; he said he had three. I told him that I might buy two of them if he could give me a better price on them, so I thought there would be some discussion. It wasn't just for the one unit. I also wanted to see and make sure that he had what he said he had."

Albert had Paulson confirm that he already had negotiated a top price of $950 per unit. If he purchased two units, the total transaction value would be $1,900. "So why did you bring extra money along with you when you already negotiated a top price of $1,900?" Albert asked. "Wouldn't you bring less and not more money if you wanted to negotiate in the parking lot as you just claimed?"

Paulson replied, "When I keep my money, I have it separated in thousands."

"So you carry thousands often then. Is that correct?" Albert asked incredulously.

Paulson quickly replied, "No, sir. But I had money at my house that I use for spending money."

"You keep that rolled in thousands?" Again, the prosecutor sounded incredulous.

Paulson simply replied, "Yes sir."

The prosecutor was definitely putting doubts in my mind. I was having a hard time grasping why the meeting didn't take place during daylight hours in a public place or at Paulson's home during the day while Joshua was at school. I was bewildered why the defendant would take more money than the asking price with him when he was hoping to negotiate a lower price. My mind was brought back to real time when I heard the prosecutor ask Paulson, "Did you think you were buying stolen PS3s?"

Paulson said, "The thought in my mind wasn't if they were stolen or not; I was just trying to buy a PlayStation 3 for my son. It's my fault. I should have put a lot more thought into what I was doing."

Prosecutor Albert continued his cross-examination, informing the jury that Paulson could have run into the company terminal and yelled out that he was being robbed. He could have yelled, "I'm being shot at. Please help! Call the police. Call 911!"

Paulson conveyed that in hindsight he could have done many things differently, but at the time he was running for his life. "My mind wasn't connecting; it wasn't making proper decisions," he said simply.

The prosecutor brought to our attention that while Paulson was hiding in the woods for quite some time, he saw a police patrol car arrive in the parking lot. Paulson confirmed that he saw the police vehicle and that he previously told the defense attorney that the reason he didn't want to talk to the police was because he was in shock.

Albert asked, "Mr. Paulson, why didn't you want to speak to the police?"

Paulson replied, "It wasn't that I didn't want to talk to them. I noticed the police car, but it didn't register. My mind was not making the connections that a person in the normal mind would make. Somebody had just put a gun in my face, threatened my life, and I had to fire a firearm, which I regret. I wish that night would have never happened."

Albert said, "Well, that is interesting you say that because in your previous testimony in 2008, you told your other attorney the reason you didn't go to the patrol car was because you didn't think the Lawrenceville Police were trustworthy. Do you recall saying that, Mr. Paulson?"

Paulson, a little frustrated and confused, said, "No, sir. I do recall saying that. Yes, I do."

Albert realized the defendant was thrown off by the last question and that he seemed unsure of how to answer it. The thought that instantly came to my mind was that this was an area of questioning that the defendant was not well-prepared for.

With a raised voice, Albert quickly continued his cross-examination by asking the defendant, "Mr. Paulson, I am seeking the truth, so please tell me and the ladies and gentlemen of the jury why you didn't stop at the police car in the parking lot. Was it because you were in shock as you stated earlier today? Or was it because you deemed the police department not trustworthy? What is your answer, sir? Were you telling the truth in 2008 or are you telling the truth now?"

Paulson looked at the prosecutor, at his defense attorney, and then at the judge with a puzzled look on his face. Edwin stood up and said, "Your Honor, there are multiple questions that the prosecutor blurted out."

Not waiting for the judge's response, Albert turned again to Paulson. "So now you're saying in 2011 that the reason you didn't talk to the police is because you weren't thinking straight?"

I was literally on the edge of my seat listening to the exchange of questions and waiting for the answers. It was a little intense for a couple of minutes, and the defendant at one point was told by the judge not to interrupt the prosecutor while he was still asking a particular question. In the end, Paulson regained his composure and admitted that he said at the previous trial that he didn't trust the police, and now he thought the reason he didn't seek out the police was because he was in shock.

I remember when the driver of the car was in the witness stand he had said something very similar when he commented that he was "taught not to trust the police." Something else that the defendant and the driver of the car had in common was the way they spoke. They seemed to share the same speech pattern and the same tone. Paulson even added "You know what I'm saying" to a few of his responses.

After Albert concluded his cross-examination, the judge released us for the evening. As I was driving home, I thought a great deal about the trial several years previously. My imagination was speculating about what had happened at that trial that warranted scheduling a retrial. I was curious if the jury had a chance to deliberate in that case, and if so, I wondered what they had decided. After giving it some more thought, I concluded that it did not matter what happened previously because I had been called to make a decision based on the facts delivered in this trial only.

When I arrived home that evening, it was very difficult not to discuss what happened in court that day with my wife, Lynda. I understood that the judge's warnings not to discuss the case with anyone were valid. If I shared something with my wife at this point in the case, she would automatically respond with a statement, and that very statement could influence the way I thought about the case and the people involved. I often wondered how many of the 13 other jurors had that kind of discipline.

I woke up Friday morning expecting to be deliberating the case sometime that day. We were told that we had a few more witnesses and then the attorneys would have their closings arguments. Of course, I didn't know how long it would take to hear the last few testimonies, but I still felt confident that by the end of this day, I would be able to discuss this case with the 11 other jurors for the first time.

Once again, I arrived early at the courthouse, not wanting to be delayed by traffic. I was the first person to arrive from our jury panel, but juror 6 arrived a few minutes later. I said hello to her, and she returned the greeting as she took the chair next to mine in the jury assembly room.

She said, "Just in case you forgot, my name is Mary Davis. I was thinking that today might be the day that the trial is completed, and we should be able to deliberate the facts. I sure hope we will finish up today so that I can spend the weekend with my husband and my two children without worrying about coming back to the courthouse on Monday morning."

I nodded in confirmation and Mary continued, "I don't mind telling you that this trial has put a strain on my marriage this week. The sooner that it is over, the sooner my family life can get back to the way it was before I received my jury summons in the mail."

I could tell Mary wanted to talk more, but our conversation was interrupted by the arrival of two more members of the jury panel. Within minutes, the rest of our group had arrived, each seemingly happy to have the trial coming to a conclusion. After a few minutes of small talk, Adams led us back into the courtroom where we took our familiar seats.

Scott Target was the next witness called to the stand by defense attorney Edwin. An uncle of driver Jared McDonald's, Target actually owned the car that was used the night of the shooting. He said he and McDonald had a close relationship.

The defense attorney had Target confirm that his nephew shared with him some of the details of what happened the night Candlestick lost his life. Edwin referenced a conversation that occurred between Target and a private investigator named Greg Bar. Target confirmed the conversation took place, but could not remember the investigator's name after all these years.

Seated in the witness stand, Target denied telling the private investigator that his nephew, McDonald, had told him that he threw the plastic gun out the window of his car before driving Candlestick to the emergency room. Target was in the witness stand less than five minutes, and at the time, I did not understand why the defense attorney even had him as a witness.

The next person called to the witness stand by Edwin was the licensed private investigator, Greg Bar, who originally had been hired by the defendant's first attorney. Bar was only on the stand for a few minutes, but he related what Target had told him in a phone conversation. McDonald told Target the meeting with Paulson was set up to rob him. The private investigator also mentioned that Target told him on the phone that McDonald confessed that he threw the gun out the window on the way to the medical center.

The hearing of the witnesses' portion of the trial was complete, but the last two people who testified contradicted each other on what the driver of the car may have verbally admitted to regarding his involvement on the night of the shooting. Although the testimony from the last two witnesses did not give me any additional evidence in my search for the truth, I remember thinking that the defense attorney had planted the seeds of doubt in our minds.

Chapter Seven

Closing Arguments

The closing arguments are considered the persuasion segment of the trial and are not considered by law to be evidence. The attorney's summations discuss the evidence that was summited in open court, but the attorneys cannot bring up issues or evidence that was not presented or accepted by the court during the trial.

The prosecuting attorney waived his right to speak, but asked the judge to reserve an opportunity to speak after the defense attorney completed his closing remarks. The judge granted Albert his request.

Edwin started his closing arguments diplomatically. "Mr. Darren Paulson and I would like to thank you for your time and energy. We would like to thank you for your dedication, and your willingness to put all of your important business and personal matters aside and give a hundred percent of your attention to this trial.

"When Darren Paulson chose you to decide his fate, he and the judge gave you an awesome amount of power that allows you to impact his immediate and distant future. You may have noticed that when the Honorable Judge Worthington enters or exits the courtroom we stand in her presence. Standing in her presence is a symbol of respect for the power of this honorable court, because the court is the giver of law.

"Ladies and gentlemen of the jury, all 14 of you command the same amount of respect. We also rose in your presence to show respect for the power you have been given by this court. Because on this date, for this week, for however long you deliberate, you're the jury that decides the facts of this case. You're the judges of the facts presented. So you, much like the honorable court, have the awesome responsibility to judge Darren Paulson."

My mind temporarily paused in an attempt to fathom this description and the authority I possessed over the life of a fellow human being. In my pursuit to listen closely to the testimonies presented by the witnesses, I had set aside the meaning of the ultimate purpose I was sitting in this jury panel box. At some point in the very near future, 12 jurors would decide if the defendant was guilty or innocent on the felony charges levied against him. And depending on how the jury members cast their votes, the defendant would either be set free or he would be incarcerated for a period of time that Judge Worthington deemed adequate.

Edwin spoke of the Bill of Indictment against Paulson. He reiterated that an indictment alone is not evidence of guilt, and he shared a potential real-life scenario to explain that point. Edwin gave an example of a homeowner who wants to put a fence around his house. He hires a surveyor and tells him, "We have neighbors, so we want to make sure the fence is on our property line. In fact, we want the fence to be about 4 feet into our property line so as not to encroach on our neighbors' land."

Next, the homeowner tells the neighbor, "Look, it's going to be a beautiful fence. It's going to be great for the both of us. We are getting a puppy and we would like to have a fenced-in yard. I'm getting a surveyor to ensure it's on my property line. Do you want to meet the surveyor? Do you have any issues?" The neighbor does not reply in a negative or positive way to the questions.

The homeowner puts up the fence and several weeks later, while eating dinner, there is a loud knock at the door. It's a sheriff's deputy, who issues the homeowner a summons and complaint about the new fence. The homeowner says, "Well, Deputy, this is wrong. I hired a surveyor, and I spoke with my neighbor before the fence was built. How did this happen?"

The deputy replies, "Just sign here please. I have other work to do." As Edwin explained, this is not the time to argue a case. This is the lawful process. This is how we resolve disputes in the United States of America.

The defense attorney continued, "The mere fact that you're sued does not mean that you put your fence on your neighbor's property. It's merely the way that the civil lawsuit gets started. The Bill of Indictment is simply the way a criminal case gets started. It's not evidence of guilt."

Edwin's example gave me a much better understanding of the legal process regarding the Bill of Indictment. The defense attorney went on to define murder with malice and forethought. He said it's an evil heart that has the intent to kill, because you have taken the life of another without justification, without mitigation, and without provocation.

Edwin gave a classic example of murder when he said, "A hit man takes money to kill me. He has no reason to kill me, except that he is hired to kill me. One day I'm walking in the courthouse and the hitman puts a bullet into my head and I die. That was not done for self-defense. That is malice murder. It's the intent to kill without justification. I wasn't doing anything to the hitman; he or she didn't have a legal right to take my life."

I visually scanned the jury panel box and found my fellow jurors focusing intently on what the defense attorney was saying. I openly admit that I appreciated how Edwin defined and broke down crucial elements and words in a manner that I could easily understand. I had to warn myself that this appreciation should in no way make me favor him over the prosecuting attorney. I had taken an oath to be a fair and impartial juror, giving favor to no one individual.

The defense attorney continued to define the next felony charge against his client. "Paulson is charged with what's called a lesser included offense, but there's nothing lesser about it except the term used is called voluntary manslaughter. Voluntary manslaughter is a crime that is not mentioned in the Bill of Indictment, but you, the juror panel, will see it on your verdict form. Voluntary manslaughter means it is murder, murder without justification.

"It's not a crime like I mentioned with the example of the hired assassin. Voluntary manslaughter is more like I come home after being in court all day and I find my wife is in bed naked with another man. What I should do is turn around and walk away from the situation. But instead, I get so enraged with passion that I go to the drawer and pull out my gun and I fire into the man who is naked in bed with my wife. At that moment, I have intent to kill. The man was not attacking me; I'm not justified in taking his life. What I am guilty of is voluntary manslaughter."

The next crime that Edwin explains is felony murder. "Felony murder is not having the intent to kill somebody. For instance, I go into a convenience store because I have no money and I desire to have whatever money they have in their cash drawer. I walk into the store with my plastic gun. The person behind the counter doesn't realize it is a plastic gun, and he reaches for his real gun. Quickly I jump over the counter top and while we are wrestling for control over the real gun, it fires a round from the chamber. By the look on the clerk's face, I can tell the bullet hit and killed him.

"I did not intend to hurt anyone, but when I put my plastic gun in that man's face, I was guilty of committing armed robbery. The store owner or clerk was justified in pulling a gun to protect himself. I set off a chain of motions to commit felony murder. Self-defense or justification is a defense to felony murder."

Edwin continued, "Aggravated assault is the next crime in the Bill of Indictment. Aggravated assault, the way it's indicted, is that Mr. Paulson, without justification, without self-defense, intentionally shot his weapon at Mr. Candlestick. So it's the intent to shoot. The person died as a result of that gunshot. So you didn't have the intent to kill, but you had the intent to shoot the person without justification. Justification obviously is a defense to the aggravated assault.

"The way we have felony murder in the indictment is you take that aggravated assault that Mr. Paulson shot Mr. Candlestick. Mr. Candlestick died as a result of that gunshot wound. If you don't believe that Mr. Paulson was either defending his life or was preventing a forcible felony and you believe that the State proved their case beyond a reasonable doubt, that's felony murder.

"But if you believe that Mr. Paulson was acting justifiably, that he was defending himself, then that's a defense for felony murder and aggravated assault, and the verdict will be not guilty.

"Possession of a gun during the commission of a felony is the last charge levied against Mr. Paulson in the Bill of Indictment. No one is saying that simply walking around with a gun in your jacket like Mr. Paulson did is a crime. The charge becomes true if you believe beyond a reasonable doubt that Mr. Paulson committed the crime of malice murder, or felony murder, or aggravated assault without justification by using a gun."

I have a college degree in political science, but I never pursued any formal education in the area of law. The pace of the trial to this point had been fast and furious, and so much information at times was given to the juror panel that I was concerned I did not comprehend all of it, especially as it pertained to the defendant being guilty or not guilty of a crime. During the first 15 minutes of the closing arguments, my mind became clearer in regards to understanding the definition of the different crimes levied against Paulson. The charges were all based upon what Paulson set in motion when he entered the back seat of McDonald's car.

The defense attorney had indicated that his client was defending himself as he was exiting the car the night Candlestick died. So what is self-defense or justification in this case? Edwin explained: "Mr. Paulson states that he was the victim of an armed robbery. Let's say that I'm walking home today from the courthouse. I'm not bothering anybody.

Suddenly, somebody comes up to me, puts a gun in my face, even if it's a replica of a gun, and they tell me to take out my wallet. I reach my hand in my pocket and I pull out my own gun and I shoot the person.

"I don't have to determine whether this person is joking around as he is waving the gun in my face. I don't have to determine if the gun is real. I don't have to determine at that very moment if the person is going to take my money and run away without hurting me. That is not how the law is written. I am a victim of a forcible felony and I have the legal right to defend myself. And that is exactly what Mr. Paulson did. Mr. Paulson used his legal right to defend himself."

Listening to Edwin conclude his closing arguments made me realize just how different this court experience was than those I'd seen on TV. I couldn't be Perry Mason attempting to solve a mystery, using investigative methods and tactics. Instead, I realized, my oath prevented me from tipping the scales toward innocence or guilt until the presiding judge directed me to do so.

I was praying for wisdom, and I remembered how King Solomon used his God-given wisdom as he pursued the truth in the case of two mothers claiming the same baby. This powerful lesson on wisdom and judgment can be found at 1 Kings 3:16-28: *16 "Then two women who were harlots came to the king and stood before him. 17 The one woman said, "Oh, my lord, this woman and I live in the same house; and I gave birth to a child while she was in the house.*

18 "It happened on the third day after I gave birth, that this woman also gave birth to a child, and we were together. There was no stranger with us in the house, only the two of us in the house. 19 "This woman's son died in the night, because she lay on it. 20 "So she arose in the middle of the night and took my son from beside me while your maidservant slept, and laid him in her bosom, and laid her dead son in my bosom.

21 "When I rose in the morning to nurse my son, behold, he was dead; but when I looked at him carefully in the morning, behold, he was not my son, whom I had borne." 22 Then the other woman said, "No! For the living one is my son, and the dead one is your son." But the first woman said, "No! For the dead one is your son, and the living one is my son." Thus they spoke before the king. 23 Then the king said, "The one says, 'This is my son who is living, and your son is the dead one'; and the other says, 'No! For your son is the dead one, and my son is the living one.'"

24 The king said, "Get me a sword." So they brought a sword before the king. 25 The king said, "Divide the living child in two, and give half to the one and half to the other." 26 Then the woman whose child was the living one spoke to the king, for ᵃshe was deeply stirred over her son and said, "Oh, my lord, give her the living child, and by no means kill him." But the other said, "He shall be neither mine nor yours; divide him!"

27 Then the king said, "Give the first woman the living child, and by no means kill him. She is his mother." 28 When all Israel heard of the judgment which the king had handed down, they feared the king, for they saw that the wisdom of God was in him to administer justice.[1]

The prosecutor now stood to make his closing argument on behalf of the State of Georgia. "The truth, ladies and gentlemen, that's why you're here today," Albert began. "That's what you expect, and that's what you deserve to hear in this case. Now, the truth is an interesting thing because the truth never changes. In this case, it's a simple definition of what actually happened. When someone doesn't tell the truth, the story changes over time.

"Someone in this case has lied. We know this to be true, because two entirely different stories are being told to you, the jury panel. Please recall that after each witness took the witness stand, they swore an oath to speak the whole truth and nothing but the truth. Shortly, it is going to be your responsibility to determine who is telling the truth, and who is not as you deliberate the actions that caused the death of Mr. Bob Candlestick.

"It will be for you to determine whether you believe a man who

---

[1] *New American Standard Bible: 1995 update.* (1995). (1 Ki 3:16–28). LaHabra, CA: The Lockman Foundation.

really has nothing to gain or lose from his testimony. This man has had no access to any of his previous statements, and his previous testimony, for over four years. And what is remarkable is that this man has told a consistent story during the two times he voluntarily gave his testimony as an eyewitness to this tragedy.

"Or, you can choose to believe someone who has had the entire case file that the State of Georgia has prepared for the same four years. Ladies and gentlemen, over those four years the defendant has had ample time to have studied and analyzed the case file over and over again.

"Let's not get hung up on this issue about whether or not there is a plastic gun involved, whether or not this was a planned robbery, because in the end, that's not the issue. Whether or not Mr. Candlestick, the man who was killed in this case, had initially done something bad, is not the issue either. For we know that the defendant sitting in this courtroom killed Mr. Candlestick. That is what we know to be true. That is an undisputed fact. And what the defense attorney has asked of you is to believe that he was justified in doing so."

Albert now gave an example of a real-life situation. "Imagine a person walking into a convenience store to rob the place by pointing a gun at the person behind the cash register. The robber gets the cash and walks toward the door to exit the convenience store. Without warning, the robber turns arounds and shoots the clerk behind the cash register. The clerk falls down and by the time the police arrive the clerk is declared deceased. He is dead.

"This is what happened in the back seat of the car that night. Mr. Darren Paulson had already decided to leave the car, and as he walked out of the car he shot and killed Mr. Candlestick. The altercation was already completed. The defendant could have just kept walking away from the vehicle with a bruised ego. But no, the defendant decided to pull out his weapon and he decided to squeeze the trigger as he stood outside the car. He made the decision to kill when he was no longer in any potential danger.

"The State's not here proclaiming that you cannot protect yourself.

The State is saying that you can only protect yourself with deadly force in the exact moment you find yourself in danger. In that moment you must believe that if you didn't use deadly force, you would die.

"Ladies and gentlemen, let me tell you what self-defense is not. There is no justification when the defendant walks away, and out of anger or out of any other motive pulls his weapon and shoots a man dead. Under the law, this type of activity is murder, and that is what the defendant committed that tragic night as Mr. Candlestick took his last breath here on earth."

Albert then told us he was glad to see the jury members taking down so many notes on the yellow legal pads furnished by the court. "It is very important that all 14 members of this jury panel have taken good notes. Do you understand what is interesting about 14 people taking notes over the course of four days? I would hazard a guess that if you were to compare what each of you has written about a particular witness, your notes will differ greatly from each other.

"Perceptions and observations of a chain of events can be dramatically different from person to person as you reflect on what you have witnessed. I remember seeing an episode on '20/20' or '48 Hours' that showed a classroom of college students. Suddenly a person ran into the classroom and stole a purse sitting on a desk. When the students were interviewed to get their statements on what had occurred, the investigators got a wide variety of descriptions of the thief.

"The students reported different ethnicities for the thief. The students described different heights and weights for the person who took the purse. When the investigators asked the students what the thief was wearing, descriptions of clothing and color varied widely. My point is that people perceive things differently. It is your responsibility as a juror to separate the chaff and the wheat and determine what you believe to be the truth as presented."

So what was the prosecuting attorney referring to when he spoke about separating the chaff from the wheat? The chaff – weeds found in the field alongside the wheat – has no nutritional value. Jesus used the chaff and the wheat in the book of Matthew to highlight the difference between believers and non-believers. The prosecuting attorney was telling members of the jury that they needed to be watchful so they could determine the good, truthful information from the bad or false information disseminated in the courtroom.

The prosecuting attorney discussed the creditability of the witnesses who testified. Albert asked the jury panel to think about, and to discuss in the deliberation room, the potential motivations behind what the witnesses said while they took the stand during the trial. He used the word 'impeachment,' and defined the term as a witness who is unworthy of belief.

The prosecutor then asked the jury panel to ponder why, if things really happened the way Paulson had described them, did McDonald not tell the police he and Candlestick were meeting with Darren Paulson to sell him a new Play Station 3. Albert said, "There would be nothing illegal about a transaction that involved selling a gaming unit. So why did Mr. McDonald tell the cops in the parking lot of the medical center the meeting was about marijuana? Why would he tell the police officers about an illegal transaction verses a legal transaction? The reason the driver of the car told the police he brokered the meeting for a buy and sell transaction of pot is, simply, because it was the truth.

"I would like to request the jury panel to think about why the defendant would deny a drug deal was occurring and instead say the meeting was about the purchase of a gaming unit? Jury members, I want you to think about the logical reasoning for the meeting among the three men. The defendant said he didn't know Mr. McDonald very well. So I ask the jury panel to ponder how Mr. McDonald became aware that Mr. Paulson was looking for a gaming unit? I want you to ask yourselves, 'How creditable is the defendant?' Do you think he is speaking the truth?

"As we listened to the testimony of the defendant, we learned that he made an annual income of around $45,000. Now that is a nice amount of money, but what I want you to also remember is that he said he keeps his money wrapped in thousands. Who keeps that kind of cash on hand on a routine basis? The defendant might have been a mechanic, but is it possible he was also a dope dealer?

"Ladies and gentlemen of the jury, we know that the defendant hid for seven weeks; he was on the run for seven weeks. That is how long it took the United States marshals to track the defendant down. When I asked the defendant why he didn't turn himself in to the police he told all of us that he was not thinking straight, and he was in shock. Ladies and gentlemen, you will have to ask yourselves if the defendant was in shock for seven weeks.

"Ladies and gentlemen of the jury, do you recall that I asked Mr. Paulson if he remembered what he told the jury panel during the previous trial about what the reason was that he didn't turn himself into the police? When the defendant could not answer my question, I reminded him that he told the members of that court that he didn't go to the police because he was taught not to trust them. Again, you must ask yourselves, 'How creditable is the defendant?'"

The prosecutor did an excellent job questioning the defendant's creditability. I wrote his questions down as quickly as I could on my yellow note pad, but I now was feeling the need to discuss them with the rest of the jury.

In fact, I was getting anxious for the trial to end so that I could start to openly discuss my thoughts with the other jury panel members. What were my fellow jurors thinking about the witnesses and the physical evidence submitted in court? I wondered if the other jurors had already made a decision about the guilt or innocence of the defendant.

My thoughts were interrupted by the prosecutor's conclusion. "It's now time for me to put this matter into your hands. It is time for you to do your duty. It's time for you to seek the truth. And the only truth you will find is that the defendant, Mr. Darren Paulson, committed murder. Mr. Paulson committed felony murder, and aggravated assault against the deceased, Mr. Bob Candlestick. Mr. Paulson is guilty of possession of a firearm during the commission of a felony three times, all of which the State has proved occurred in Gwinnett County.

"It has been a long trial, and I want to thank you for your personal sacrifice. I want to thank you for seeking the truth. The State of Georgia asks you to find the defendant guilty on all charges. Thank you very much."

Chapter Eight

The Judge Addresses the Jury Panel

We were all restless and anxious to move on to the deliberation portion of this case. There was a lot of speculation on my part regarding how the 12 of us would begin the process of expressing our beliefs and perceptions around it.

First, though, we heard from the judge about the law and the boundaries that we had to stay within as jurors. As the judge spoke, I realized how important it is to know the law before passing judgment.

The judge reminded us that we were considering the case of the State of Georgia versus Darren Paulson. The Grand Jury of Gwinnett County had returned a Bill of Indictment charging Paulson with the offenses of murder, felony murder, and aggravated assault, and three counts of possession of a firearm during the commission of a felony. We would have the indictment in the deliberation room so that we could read and examine it carefully and see exactly the way and manner in which the State brought these allegations against Paulson.

The judge advised us that as far as a plea regarding this Bill of Indictment was concerned, Paulson had entered a plea of not guilty. She cautioned us to the fact that an indictment was not evidence of guilt, and that Paulson was presumed to be innocent until proven guilty.

"Mr. Paulson enters upon the trial of the case with a presumption of innocence in his favor," Judge Worthington said. "The presumption of innocence, it surrounds him, it protects him, and it clothes him. It remains with Mr. Paulson until it is overcome by the State with evidence that is sufficient to convince you, the jury, beyond a reasonable doubt, that Mr. Paulson is guilty of the offense charged. The law says no person shall be convicted of any crime unless and until each element of the crime is proven beyond a reasonable doubt.

"The burden of proof rests upon the State to prove every material allegation of the indictment and every essential element of the crime charged, beyond a reasonable doubt. There is no burden of proof whatsoever upon Mr. Paulson and the burden never shifts to Mr. Paulson to prove his innocence. When a defense, such as self-defense, is raised by the evidence, the burden is on the State to negate or disprove it beyond a reasonable doubt.

"However, the State is not required to prove the guilt of the accused beyond all doubt, or to a mathematical certainty. A reasonable doubt means just what it says. A reasonable doubt is a doubt of a fair-minded, impartial juror who is honestly seeking truth. A reasonable doubt is a doubt based upon common sense and reason. It is not a vague or arbitrary doubt, but a reasonable doubt is a doubt for which a reason can be given. It may arise from a consideration of the evidence or a lack of evidence, a conflict in the evidence, or any combination of these.

"If you, as a member of the jury, after giving careful consideration to all the facts and circumstances of this case, find your minds are wavering, unsettled or unsatisfied, then that is a doubt of the law, and you should acquit Mr. Paulson. To acquit him means to find him not guilty of an individual charge, or all charges brought against him.

"If that doubt does not exist in your minds as to the guilt of the accused, then you are authorized to convict him. To convict him means to find him guilty of an individual charge, or all charges brought against him. Just remember, if the State fails to prove Mr. Paulson's guilt beyond a reasonable doubt, it would be your duty to acquit Mr. Paulson."

The judge reminded us about another optional charge that was not listed in the original Bill of Indictment. She referred us to Count 1 murder and Count 2 felony murder and mentioned that after consideration of all the evidence, before we would be authorized to return a verdict of guilty of malice murder or felony murder, we must first determine whether mitigating circumstances, if any, would cause the offense to be reduced to voluntary manslaughter.

She mentioned that we would have a verdict form with us, and after we had reached a unanimous verdict, we would have to write it directly on that verdict form. The judge told us, "Take some time to review the verdict form in its entirety, viewing all the options before you begin marking it with your decisions. Whatever the unanimous verdict would turn out to be, you need to record it directly on the verdict form, and then the verdict form would be returned and published in open court."

Regarding the verdict form, she instructed us that we must make a determination as to each count separately, and there was no requirement that our verdict be the same on each count. Our verdict could be different as to some of the counts, or it could be the same on all counts.

The judge said, "You are only concerned with the guilt or innocence of Mr. Paulson. You are not to concern yourselves with any possible or potential issues of punishment. In deciding this case, you should not be influenced by sympathy or prejudice. It is your duty to consider the facts objectively without favor or affection.

"Whatever your verdict is, it must be unanimous, that is, agreed by all. The verdict must be signed by one of your members as foreperson, dated and returned to be published in open court."

The judge mentioned that our first duty as we deliberated was to select one person who would act as the foreperson, who would preside over the deliberations and sign the verdict form to which all 12 jury members would freely and voluntarily agree. The judge cautioned us to start the deliberations with an open mind and that we should consult with one another and consider each other's views and opinions.

I had temporarily forgotten that there were 14 members of our jury panel until the judge assigned Vince Botta and Nancy Nokomis as the alternate jurors. I understood that the court needed extra juror members in case one of us could not complete the trial, but I felt sad for the alternates because they had invested so much time but would not have the opportunity to deliberate the facts in the case. They were taken upstairs separately.

The judge cautioned us that we should proceed with electing the foreperson, but that we shouldn't begin deliberations until we received the evidence, the verdict form, and the copy of the indictment. The bailiff then escorted us to the deliberation room and said he would be right back to take us to the cafeteria for lunch. Just as we thought we were finally able to discuss the case, we were told to wait just a little longer!

Chapter Nine

How do you Vote?
What is your Verdict?

Was your mind perfectly impartial as you read about the case? You now have all the information you need to make your decision!

Unfortunately, you do not have the benefit of looking at any physical evidence, such as the photographs and other items marked as evidence and brought into the courtroom. Nor do you have the benefit of looking the witnesses in their eyes and watching their body language while they shared their testimony. You also do not have the benefit of going into the deliberation room with some of the evidence and discussing the case with 11 other people who saw and heard everything you did. With that said, have you come to a conclusion?

Before you read the next chapter that explains what happened in the deliberation room, please go to our website, www.juror11.com, and vote "guilty" or "not guilty" on the six felony charges levied against Darren Paulson via our electronic verdict form. Once you start reading the next few chapters, you will be able to compare your thoughts with our thoughts, and your verdict with our verdict.

I am interested in finding out when you made up your mind. At what point did you feel you knew how to cast your vote? What chapter or what witness allowed you to have the clarity to choose guilty or not guilty on the charges levied against Paulson?

I look forward to reading your remarks. You are invited to leave any comments you would like to share about the book on our Facebook page. https://www.facebook.com/juror11/

Chapter Ten

Jury Deliberations

Adams, the court bailiff, escorted us to the jury deliberation room. Once we arrived in the room, he closed the door and said he would be back shortly with a copy of the charges, the indictment, and the physical evidence. The judge told us that we could not discuss the case before the documents arrived.

In the meantime, I asked the group as a whole if anyone wanted to volunteer to be the foreperson. I am not sure who said it first, but several people, without hesitation, said I should be the foreperson. After I accepted the responsibility, Sang, an older woman who had not spoken much previously, asked the jury panel for clarification. "Does everyone agree to have Terry as our foreperson?"

I didn't vote, of course, but all 11 juror members either nodded their heads or verbally agreed that I should take the position.

Not long afterward, the bailiff came back into the room, and I asked him to take us to lunch early. No one wanted to deliberate for 30 minutes and then take a lunch break. We ate our lunch in a private area not far from the cafeteria. I didn't realize why we were dining in a private area until it dawned on me later that the court didn't want us to have a chance to speak with anyone else in the "outside world," even if that only amounted to the cafeteria.

During our lunch, it was obvious that we were all eager to get back into the deliberation room to finally start discussing the case. The situation reminded me of childhood, and the anticipation I always felt on Christmas Eve not knowing exactly what would be under the tree. We finished our lunches quickly, and were ready to return to the deliberation room after about 15 minutes, but we had to wait until the bailiffs finished their lunches. We watched them swallow their food, one bite at a time, almost in slow motion. One of the jury members told me to ask the bailiffs to hurry up and finish their lunch so we could begin deliberating, but I declined to do so.

Like the other jurors, I was restless and excited about the conversations that I would be having in just a matter of minutes. I was wondering if the other jurors' opinions would be similar to mine. I questioned if we would all get along and be respectful of one another. How long would it take to complete our discussions?

It seemed a million questions were floating around in my mind. But many would be answered soon, because the bailiff was finally opening the door to the jury deliberation room.

The jury room had one conference table and 12 comfortable chairs with wheels. The back wall was full of windows overlooking the back parking lot of the courthouse. There was a small bathroom that had an uncontrollable drip that eventually got on several jurors' nerves. Every time there was silence in the room, we heard this drip; three seconds later, we heard the drip again. A whiteboard with markers was on one of the side walls.

I took a seat in the middle of the table with my back to the windows overlooking the parking lot. I started the deliberations by stating to everyone that I really did not know how to begin. Then I said, "Let's go around the table and make sure that everyone understands the charges and the definition of the crimes."

It only took about 10 seconds before everyone was sharing their thoughts and asking questions about the law as it was defined by the judge. After 20 or 30 minutes of discussions with no real direction, I stood up, and went to the whiteboard.

The first thing I wrote on the whiteboard was, "Do we believe the plastic handgun was used in the car?" I placed a 'yes' or 'no' next to this question, and everyone immediately agreed that the gun was linked to the scene, so I circled the word 'yes'.

The next question I wrote on the whiteboard was, "Do you believe that Bob Candlestick assaulted Darren Paulson?" Everyone agreed that one of the very first things that happened in that car was that Candlestick reached around into the back seat, grabbed Paulson by the collar, and pointed the gun to his forehead. I circled the word 'yes' again after verifying that everyone was in agreement.

The third question I wrote on the whiteboard was, "Do you believe that Paulson was afraid for his life while sitting in the back seat of the car?" Like the second question, this question was answered in a minute or so, in the affirmative. Before I moved on, however, I confirmed once again that everyone agreed Paulson was afraid for his life while sitting in the back seat of the car. Once again, without hesitation, everyone answered 'yes'.

I said, "When a person fears for their life, according to the law, they do have justification to protect themselves even if it means taking a human life in the process." By the shaking of the jurors' heads, it became pretty obvious that everyone thought there was a valid self-defense claim in this case. And according to the answers to the questions written on the whiteboard, there was reason to acquit Paulson.

Before I could say another word, Mary raised her hand and asked, "Does this mean the defendant is not guilty on all charges?"

"Yes, if we believe that Paulson was fearful for his life, then self-defense, according to the information we were given by the judge, is the correct option," I replied. "Because self-defense is our belief, we have to find Paulson not guilty on all counts."

Mary said very clearly, "No, he is guilty of something. He should have never shot that man; he should have just kept running. What about voluntary manslaughter? Is he not guilty of that charge?"

Obviously, something in the case was troubling Mary, in almost a personal way. I responded, "No, not if he was fearful for his life, and was acting in self-defense." I started to think Mary was having a personal issue with the defendant possibly being acquitted. Something was very troubling to Mary, and all of a sudden the outcome of this case seemed very personal to her. I reminded everyone of the example the defense attorney gave us to define voluntary manslaughter, and that it was a crime of passion.

Another minute or so passed in silence, as Mary thought about my answer. I and the rest of the juror panel could tell Mary was trying to figure everything out in her head. The 12 of us had been deliberating for a total of 45 minutes at this point.

Mary then said, "No way, he is guilty. He cannot get off without any punishment. There is a man dead, and someone has to pay. Paulson should have kept walking or running and not fired his gun. Because of him, there is someone dead; someone has to pay."

Just minutes before Mary shared her thoughts and comments, I noticed she was looking at the pictures from the crime scene. I saw her going back to the only picture we had of the dead man. The picture showed him lying on his back on a metal bed with his eyes open. Even though the picture of him was completely lifeless, we could tell he was a handsome man with striking physical features.

When Mary spoke the words "someone died; someone has to pay," I looked around the table at the other jurors to see their reactions. Some jurors had looks of amazement on their faces, while others seemed stunned.

Before I could say anything about her statement, Sam Nichols, who was the oldest member of our jury panel, spoke out loud for the first time. "I agree. Paulson should have kept running without firing his weapon."

Now there were two members of the jury who believed that Paulson should have kept running without discharging his pistol and ultimately killing Candlestick. I said, "I think all of us would agree with you, Mary and Sam, the best decision Paulson could have made that night was to have kept running without discharging his weapon.

"But let's take it one step further and say the best decision Paulson could have made was to not answer the phone when McDonald called him to schedule the meeting. Because he did not make that decision, we now have the responsibility as the jury panel to filter through the evidence. We are charged to make our decision based on the evidence, and inform the judge if our verdict finds Paulson to be innocent or guilty."

After another 30 minutes or so of general discussion, I asked if everyone thought it might be helpful for us to do a role play to get a better visual idea of spacing, timing, and emotions. Paulson's attorney had done a mock setup in the courtroom, and everyone agreed that it would be helpful to try to recreate the scene that night for ourselves.

I asked jurors Marvin and Shelby if they would participate in the role play, and they agreed. I placed two of our chairs as if they were the front seats in the Chevy Caprice Classic. I placed a third chair positioned behind the driver's seat where Paulson would have sat in the car that night.

Shelby sat in the supposed back seat, Marvin was in the front passenger seat, and I gave him the plastic gun. As soon as I walked away, he grabbed Shelby by the shirt and pointed the gun to his forehead, saying, "Hey, scumbag, give me your money, or I am going to kill you."

Shelby was a little startled, but he gained his composure quickly and said, "You got it, you got it." He put his hands up, and with his right hand reached into his pocket to pull out his imaginary $2,000 and put it onto the imaginary rear seat to his right. Marvin reached for the fake money, and Shelby got out of his chair and simulated pulling out his imaginary gun, firing a shot as he was leaving the car.

It took 20 seconds to complete the role play. Everyone in the room was a little shook up because the jurors were intense as they simulated what might have happened in the car that tragic night. I believe we all gave a sigh of relief when they finished, and several minutes passed before our hearts calmed down to a normal beat per minute.

The role play gave us a very good visual in regards to physical placement of the people in the car as well as their potential body movements as described in the trial.

I looked at Sam who, just a few minutes before, said he believed Paulson should have kept running. I asked him, "Do you think it is possible for Paulson to think his life was at risk even as he was leaving the car?"

As Sam mulled the question, I went into a little role playing myself. "Sam, as the door opened, and Paulson was getting ready to exit the car, the dome light came on.

"We know, based on testimony from the medical examiner, and the weapons expert, that Candlestick reached with his left hand for Paulson. We know this because the bullet that came from Paulson's gun went through Candlestick's left wrist before lodging into the left side of his chest. This is the pathway of the bullet explained to us by the medical examiner."

I asked Sam if he agreed that Candlestick was reaching for Paulson with his left hand when the dome light came on as Paulson was trying to escape. I said, "Is it possible that what Paulson saw was Candlestick reaching for him with one hand and perhaps the plastic gun in the other hand? Do you think it is possible that Paulson thought Candlestick was going to shoot him while he was exiting the car?" I had asked the questions in a rapid fire sequence, but I now waited for Sam to reply.

Sam tossed the questions around in his mind for nearly a minute before replying. "Yes, it is possible that Paulson thought he was going to get shot."

I asked, "Do you think that the fear of losing his life, which we all agreed on earlier, is what Paulson felt while he was sitting in the back seat of that car?"

Sam replied, "Yes." I could feel the excitement in the room because it seemed we were getting closer to a consensus. The role playing and the discussion had convinced Sam that Paulson had justification to protect himself, even with a deadly weapon.

Everyone in the room was excited to see the change in Sam's thought process from focusing on what Paulson should have done to what he might be feeling in the back seat. Any reasonable person in the same situation would have been afraid for his life.

We all agreed that we did not know for certain why the three men were meeting, whether it was about a PlayStation 3 or a couple of pounds of marijuana. In addition, McDonald and Candlestick could have arranged an armed robbery. With any of those scenarios, it was obvious that the role play put everyone on a heightened alert level.

With our hopes high, I turned to Mary and asked her, "Do you think it is possible for Paulson to think his life was in danger as he was exiting the car?"

Mary simply said, "While he was exiting the car, no." This question was slightly different than the question I asked on the whiteboard. The question I posed on the whiteboard was: Do you believe that Paulson was afraid for his life while sitting in the back seat of the car?

Immediately after Mary's reply, one of the jurors vehemently said, "You've got to be kidding." Groans and whispers could be heard from others. Someone asked Mary to refresh their memory by restating her position.

Mary replied, "Paulson should have kept running when he got out of the car." I could tell the other jurors were filled with disappointment, frustration, and even disgust. It was inconceivable to 11 of us that Mary didn't believe there was even a possibility that Paulson was afraid for his life while he was exiting the car.

We explained it did not matter what we thought should have happened in the case. "For you, Mary, to deny that it is not even remotely possible for Paulson to be afraid for his life is unimaginable to us," I told her.

Tensions were extremely high. We had just witnessed Sam changing his mind because of the visual he received during the reenactment of the shooting, but Mary's beliefs did not seem to be impacted whatsoever.

I really didn't know how to proceed. But as the foreperson, it also was my responsibility to see that all of the jurors had the opportunity to share their thoughts without being pounced upon or personally ridiculed – even if those thoughts sounded ridiculous to some or all of us. For that reason, I decided to ask the jurors to raise their hands and be recognized by me before they answered a question, asked a question, or made a general statement.

After a few minutes of silence to get our breathing back to normal, Sang raised her hand and asked Mary, "Have you ever been mad at your husband for something he did to you, or mad at him because he made a dumb decision without discussing it with you?" Mary nodded her head with a slight smile of what appeared to be agreement.

Sang asked, "When you got mad at him, even though he may have said he was sorry for whatever it was that got you mad at him, were you still mad at him for a while?" The rest of us sat up slightly, waiting for Mary's response to the question. Again, Mary smiled as if in agreement, although she still did not answer the question out loud.

Mary seemed to realize – as we all did – that by answering the question truthfully she would be contradicting her earlier statement that Paulson's emotions somehow changed from fearing for his life to anger and retaliation in a matter of a second or two.

After several minutes of silence, one of the members of the jury said, "Do you really want us to believe that you can control your emotions so easily?"

Mary had no response.

My own thoughts flashed back to a time when my wife was mad at me for making a financial decision without first discussing it with her. The decision was the correct one, but that was not her point. After our heated discussion I apologized and agreed she was right. "Now, can we get back to normal and move on with our day?" I asked her.

"Terry, it just doesn't work that way," Lynda replied. "Just because you say you're sorry does not mean I am no longer upset with you, just like that." It literally took her half a day before I felt her complete forgiveness.

Now, in the jury room, one of the other women said to Mary, "When

I get mad at my husband for whatever reason, my anger usually lingers on for minutes and sometimes hours, and even sometimes a day or so before I am able to put it behind me."

Mary heard her, but she slowly and deliberately turned her chair so it was facing the wall rather than the people in the room. Obviously, Mary could not or did not want to explain why she was holding out for voluntary manslaughter.

The group's frustration level had peaked again. Mary had just defied logic in regards to a relationship between a husband and wife. Calmly, I stood up and asked her, "What other emotions do you think can be controlled or can change in a matter of a single second or a few seconds?"

Mary thought for a few minutes before responding with a single word, "Happiness."

I continued, "Let's review what we are talking about in regards to what happened in the car and how it relates to the emotions of fear and anger." I was standing next to the whiteboard that was at the end of the table. "Most of us agree that that it is possible beyond a reasonable doubt that Paulson was afraid he might die, and that fear continued to be present even as he was exiting the Caprice Classic."

I turned to Mary. "You, on the other hand, believe that Paulson was afraid in the back seat, but as soon as he opened the door and the dome light came on, and when he took his first step outside the car, his emotions changed from fear to anger. Do you really think it is possible that a person's emotions can go from fear to anger just as quickly and easily as me turning off the lights in this room?"

At that moment, I reached over to the light switch and turned off the lights, and we all sat quietly in the dark for a brief period of time. The room was completely silent in anticipation of hearing Mary's response to the question, but she said nothing. I flipped the light switch again, the lights came back on, and I said, "This is anger," and I flipped the light switch again to turn off the lights. "This represents fear," I said.

I asked Mary, "Do you really believe that you can go from fearing for your life to being angry with revenge on your mind in the amount of time it takes me to turn the lights on and off?" Then, I flipped the switch one more time on and off to show how quickly the atmosphere in the room changed. The silence was dramatic. Many of the jurors were on the edge of their seats in anticipation of Mary's answer.

After perhaps a minute or two, Mary responded. "I do believe that a person could change from being afraid to being angry very quickly, just like turning the light switch on and off."

The group sighed loudly once again. I asked everyone to calm down, and then I asked the rest of the jurors if they thought it was a possibility that Paulson could change his emotions from fear to anger so quickly. Everyone agreed that it might be possible, although not likely.

I said to Mary, "The group agrees with you that it is possible to change emotions quickly, so if they can agree that it is possible to change emotions so quickly, do you think it is a possibility that fear could also linger for several minutes? And more specifically, as Paulson was leaving the vehicle do you think that it is possible that fear was the dominant emotion?"

Without hesitation, Mary responded. "No, it is not a possibility. My faith is so strong that I do not become afraid."

With this statement, many in the room threw up their hands in disgust and disbelief. Marvin said something about Mary's faith, which I could not hear clearly over the noise of everyone releasing their discontentment. Mary, too, heard Marvin, and she swung her chair around to face him. "What did you say?" she said, and before our eyes her face transformed from a look of stubbornness to what I can only describe as hatred. The transformation of her face startled me.

Marvin did not repeat his statement, so I decided it was time to take a break. The conversation was getting heated and out of control – others in the group were chatting amongst themselves, using words like "ridiculous" and "she's lying" – and I was afraid things were going to get even more personal. I called the bailiff and asked if we could take a break and get some drinks or snacks.

The bailiff told us the cafeteria was already closed – it was a little after 5 p.m. – but he could take us to the vending machines. I was not really looking to buy anything; I just wanted to get out of the room and leave the craziness of our discussions for a few minutes.

During the break, five people stayed in the room, three went to the restroom down the hall, and four of us went upstairs to the vending machines. Although I was glad to leave the room, I wondered what I was going to say when we all began deliberating again.

We made awkward small talk as we walked to the vending machines, but everyone's minds were on Mary and what she was thinking. I had a few minutes alone while we were on break and I thought about what Mary had said concerning her faith and how that did not allow her to be afraid.

I consider myself a pretty strong Christian and a man of solid faith. I have taught Bible studies to children and led some of our church's small community groups, and I even undertook a seven-year study of the Bible. So, I tried to remember times I had been afraid, and what my faith had taught me.

One of those times was after a storm, when we had lost a few shingles off our roof. Since I don't like heights, and I had never been on our roof before, I had lined up a friend to replace the shingles. When we realized another storm was coming, and my friend couldn't help for a few days, I decided to do the work myself.

I got our 28-foot ladder, put it on our deck, and asked Lynda to hold the ladder as best she could. I climbed to the top, and had a little trouble getting off the ladder and taking my first few steps onto the roof. I walked in front of our fireplace stack because I thought that if I lost my footing, perhaps I would slide into the chimney instead of off the roof and onto the back deck. I literally had to climb all the way to the top because the missing shingles were two feet on the other side of the top ridge line.

I climbed carefully to the top and put one leg on the left side and one on the right side of the center roof line. My hammer and replacement shingles were in a backpack and as I was getting them out, I looked around. The storm was coming in quickly, the wind had picked up, and I felt a little afraid. After saying a quick prayer, I finished the job and managed to safely return to the deck.

I cannot say that my faith in God prevented me from being afraid. Although faith in God prevents us from living in fear on a daily basis, my faith won't prevent me from ever being afraid. Take the time Peter walked on water toward Jesus, found in Matthew 14:26-33: *26 When the disciples saw him walking on the water, they were terrified. In their fear, they cried out "It's a ghost!" 27 But Jesus spoke to them at once. "Don't be afraid," he said. "Take courage, I am here!" 28 Then Peter called to him, "Lord, if it's really you, tell me to come to you, walking on the water." 29 "Yes, Come," Jesus said. So Peter went over the side of the boat and walked on the water toward Jesus. 30 But when he saw the strong wind and waves, he was terrified and began to sink. "Save me, Lord!" he shouted. 31 Jesus immediately reached out and grabbed him. "You have so little faith," Jesus said. "Why did you doubt me?" 32 When they climbed back into the boat, the wind stopped. 33 Then the disciples worshiped him. "You really are the Son of God!" they exclaimed.*

Peter, who was in the presence of Jesus Christ, was startled by the wind and became afraid. Peter's faith was not perfectly stable, and as a result, he began to sink. I thought to myself, how could Mary's faith be so solid that she never experienced fear? Perhaps she actually sometimes did experience fear, but she just could not admit it because she wanted Paulson to be punished for a crime that she deemed needed payment.

Perhaps in her heart, she really did believe that because someone died, someone had to pay. I vividly remembered Mary making this statement while we were answering the questions on the whiteboard, about 45 minutes into our deliberations.

It was about 5:30 p.m. as we headed back to the deliberation room. The courthouse seemed eerily quiet, since most employees had left for the day. We walked through the room where earlier that day about 150 people had waited to be sent on to jury panels.

Back in the deliberation room, I hoped that some of the tension had been released. Instead, I quickly learned, it had intensified. I had not even said a single word when Marvin said, "I think we have a hung jury here, Terry."

I felt it was too early to come to that conclusion, and I turned to Mary, asking if she thought it was a hung jury.

"At this point, I have not heard anything to change my current decision," Mary replied.

Rosemary gasped in disappointment. Mary quickly swung her swivel chair around toward her, and her face transformed to a look of hatred. "I heard you when I was in the restroom when you were here talking with the others," Mary said angrily. "You thought I did not hear you, but I heard every word."

At first Rosemary was taken aback with surprise that she had been overheard, but then after a brief moment, she said, "I have nothing to hide from you or the rest of the group who were not here during the break. What I told the others is the truth. I can tell you are shutting down. Your body language says it all, and you are now turning in your swivel chair and placing your back to us more and more. You refuse to answer a lot of the questions because you are simply shutting yourself down."

Mary fired back a few comments and denied that she was shutting down, saying simply she did not have a lot to say at this point. She concluded this heated exchange by saying, "You have your interpretations, and I have mine."

I could tell that the other jurors felt as Rosemary did, and I asked God to help me guide our discussion and bring some harmony to our group of 12. I decided to focus on reasonable doubt and the foundation of our judiciary system – that every person is presumed innocent until proven guilty. With that said, we as a jury panel started to review the facts again to determine what the prosecutor proved that eliminated reasonable doubt.

We started at the beginning, and some of us felt a renewed sense of energy, because Mary reengaged and we reviewed the case evidence. In my opinion, we had to focus on the facts and the evidence that was submitted, and not just react with our emotions and feelings.

This dialogue made us review our notes, and about 30 minutes into this productive discussion, I asked Mary, "Did the prosecutor prove beyond a reasonable doubt that Paulson left the car and proceeded to attempt to kill the people in the car? What did the prosecutor do or say specifically that proved beyond a reasonable doubt that Paulson wanted revenge?"

Mary said, "Yes, the prosecutor did prove beyond a reasonable doubt that Paulson wanted to kill Candlestick because he roughed him up and stole his money."

We all gasped again. By denying that a reasonable doubt could exist in this scenario, Mary seemed determined to turn away from what we considered the truth.

The jury panel was exhausted. Bailiff Adams knocked on the door and brought in a note from the judge. I read what the judge had written and asked my fellow jurors if we should order food, which would take about an hour. Everyone said no, it was pointless to stay any longer. Mary was not going to change her mind, so we were a hung jury. I stopped further discussion and asked Adams if we could have a few more minutes alone before we answered the judge.

After the bailiff left the room, several people started talking at once. The frustration was present in everyone's voice, except Mary's. Many wanted to throw in the towel, call it a hung jury, go home, and be done with the process. Finally, Shelby spoke up. "I took an oath, and I am going to take it seriously. I do not want to give up quite yet."

After a few more minutes of discussion, I asked Mary, "Do you think you might have a change of heart or possibly decide to change your opinion on how you would vote on the charges against Paulson?"

Mary answered, "It is possible, but as of right now, I still come to the same conclusion as before – guilty of manslaughter."

I asked again, "Mary, to make sure we are clear, I am going to ask you the question again. Do you think you could possibly have a different answer than you currently do now?"

Mary said, "Yes, Terry, it is possible." At the same time, she nodded her head in a sign of affirmation.

Knowing it had been a long week for everyone, and it was Friday evening, I said to the jury, "Why don't we skip the dinner, call it a day, and come back on Monday? That will give us the weekend to think things over. Several of you have already mentioned that you think we should quit and inform the judge we do not all agree on the verdict. I do not want to come back, but I also remember taking an oath, and I know how serious this situation is, so I would like to stop now and resume on Monday morning."

Everyone finally agreed, and I called the bailiff back in the room. I handed him the note I wrote to the judge indicating that we did not want to have dinner and we would like to break for the weekend and resume on Monday morning. Shortly thereafter, the judge called us back to the courtroom with defendant Paulson and both attorneys present.

The judge said that she understood our request. She mentioned that she had another trial beginning on Monday and would be going through the jury selection for that trial. She told us to report to the courtroom at 9 a.m. Then she reminded us that we should not read, research, or discuss anything that had to do with this case.

After we were dismissed, we were ushered back to the jury deliberation room to pick up our belongings, and then the bailiff led us out to the main hallway. Not very many words were spoken during the walk through the corridor. Everyone just wanted to get out of there before exploding in frustration or saying something mean or personal to Mary.

Chapter Eleven

A Weekend with Juror 11

Walking out of the courthouse that Friday evening, I was filled with mixed emotions that, quite candidly, had drained me of my energy. It was hard for me to wrap my mind around what was happening in the deliberation room with juror number 6. I felt I was witnessing a person who wanted to be both judge and executioner of the defendant in this murder trial!

And as foreperson, I felt the full weight of the judicial process on my shoulders. I felt responsible to the judge, the attorneys, the defendant on trial, and the members of the jury panel who had elected me as their foreperson. I felt helpless to steer the outcome desired for the 10 other jurors who took an oath, like I did, to follow the law given by the judge presiding over this case. We were charged to treat the defendant as innocent until proven guilty beyond a reasonable doubt.

During dinner that evening with Lynda, I told her I had to return to the courthouse on Monday. I did not mention any of the details to her, but she could tell that my thoughts were consumed by the trial. Lynda and I finished our meal and then watched a movie, but my mind kept returning to the trial.

I spent Saturday catching up on some paperwork for our business, but the trial preoccupied my thoughts. I pondered how I would start the conversation with the other jurors on Monday morning, and I wondered what I could have done differently Friday afternoon during deliberations. What approach had I not taken that possibly could have led Mary to the same verdict that 11 of her peers already had chosen? I searched my mind for a tactic, a statement, or an action I could perform that would bring about a unanimous decision of not guilty.

I reflected again on Mary's statement about faith and fear. Being afraid was a huge part of this case, because if Paulson was truly afraid for his life, he did in fact have justification to protect himself. I decided to look up the word "fear" in the dictionary to review it for myself and perhaps have something to share with the rest of the jurors on Monday morning.

According to Wikipedia, fear is a distressing, negative emotion induced by a perceived threat. It is a basic survival mechanism occurring in response to a specific stimulus, such as pain or the threat of danger. In short, fear is the ability to recognize danger and flee from it or confront it, also known as the "fight or flight response." Fear should be distinguished from the related emotional state of anxiety, which typically occurs without any external threat.

Additionally, Wikipedia stated that fear is related to the specific behaviors of escape and avoidance, whereas anxiety is the result of threats that are perceived to be uncontrollable or unavoidable. Worth noting is that fear almost always relates to future events, such as the worsening or continuation of a situation that is unacceptable. Fear also could be an instant reaction to something presently happening.

In the Paulson trial, the defendant clearly wanted to get out of the back seat alive. Every member of the jury had tried to no avail to explain to Mary about the potential emotions that were being experienced inside the car that night. I began to wonder if we had a vigilante on the jury panel.

I went to sleep Saturday evening without a clear plan on how to lead the deliberations come Monday morning. Not having an action plan made me sad, not only for myself, but for my fellow jurors because, with a hung jury, we would not be upholding the law as the judge had explained it to us.

On Sunday afternoon, I came to the conclusion that Mary most likely would not change her mind. I thought about how in the very beginning of our deliberation she sided with us, up to the moment where she realized Paulson would be found not guilty on all counts. Since everyone else in the room had to have seen Mary's transformation, I needed to do something extraordinary or we would all experience an injustice brought on by juror number six.

I do not pretend to know the law, and I was not sure if anything would change, but I felt compelled as the foreman of this jury panel to share with the judge what I saw and experienced. The only thing I did know for sure was that we had two alternate jurors sitting in the jury assembly room while we were deliberating. The two alternates could not be dismissed until the case had come to a conclusion. Perhaps the judge could take Mary off the jury panel and put an alternate in her place.

This was my thought, so I sat down in my basement office and started to write a letter addressed to the judge. In the letter I highlighted that early on the in the deliberations the jury panel witnessed Mary change her answers so that the charge of voluntary manslaughter could be attached to the defendant. I included in the letter many of the details that took place until the moment we left the deliberation room Friday evening.

I now had an action plan for Monday morning. I decided that I would start by breaking the jury panel into three groups. All of us, group by group, would re-read the 11-page Charge of the Court document. This document is what the judge gave us just before we were sent to deliberate.

The Charge of the Court document explained the charges as well as defined the law by the different crimes levied against the defendant. By reading the document out loud, I could be certain that everyone truly understood the charges and the definition of those charges before we made our formal vote.

If Mary's opinion had not changed by the time we finished reading the document, then I would bring out the two-page letter I had written to the judge. Assuming the other jurors agreed with the letter's content, I would ask if we should submit it to the judge. Hopefully the judge could determine if we had any other options to stop the injustice we felt was occurring in the deliberation room.

Chapter Twelve

A Weekend with Juror 6

Mary was grateful that deliberations had ended for the day. She was also very happy that she was able to fend off the other members of the jury panel and not be persuaded to change her mind from assigning the charge of manslaughter to Paulson. Mary prayed to God she would be able to have the same success at home with her husband.

Ricky was sure to ask questions about her day in the courthouse, but she knew he would also respect the judge's order not to discuss the details of the case with anyone. Ultimately, she decided to tell her husband that by Monday evening she hoped to be able to discuss the case with him.

As Mary pulled into her driveway, she saw her husband and children getting out of Ricky's car, the children carrying buckets of chicken. She was grateful that she did not have to cook for everyone because she was emotionally exhausted from being in the deliberation room nearly all day.

She opened her car door, and the kids rushed up. Bobby yelled, "We knew you'd be tired, Mom, so we brought dinner. But hurry so we can eat it while it's hot, and you can tell us what happened in the murder trial today."

Ricky gathered everyone around the table and asked them to bow their heads in prayer. "Heavenly Father, we thank you for the food we are about to receive and we thank you for our healthy bodies. Father, I ask you in your precious son's name, Jesus Christ, to fill our hearts with purity, peace, love, and happiness. Please Lord God, fill our minds with your wisdom and give us clarity so we know and understand right from wrong, so we can bring you glory in everything we do. Again, we pray for these things in the name of Jesus Christ, Amen!"

Mary and the children exchanged inquisitive looks because the prayer was quite different from Ricky's normal dinnertime invocation. As Mary began to pass around the food, Bobby spoke up excitedly. "Tell us about the trial! What happened?"

Mary explained that she had to go back to the courthouse on Monday morning and that the 12 jurors were still reviewing the evidence and discussing whether or not the defendant was guilty of some of the charges filed against him or not guilty of all charges. Mary said the decision was a difficult one, but she felt confident that Monday would be her last day on the jury panel and that Monday evening she would be able to talk more about the trial with her family. She finished by saying, "So for now, the judge asked us not to share any of the details of the case with anyone, including our curious children."

While she spoke, Ricky looked at Mary with suspicious eyes, but now he turned his attention to the children and asked how their days had gone at school.

After dinner, Ricky and Mary cleared the table in awkward silence. Finally, Ricky told Mary he had to go to the office on Saturday to work on a project, and Mary said that would give her time to catch up on some housework that needed to be done. With that said, Ricky retired upstairs to his home office, and Mary sat down at the table again to call her best friend, Janet.

When Mary explained she had been on the jury panel of a murder trial, Janet was surprised. "I haven't heard from you all week. This was the first I knew about that," Janet proclaimed.

"I know, and please forgive me for not calling. It's been a very hectic week for me," Mary said. Then she told Janet about the tension in her marriage due to the trial.

Janet said, "You're forgiven for not calling, but how in the world did you ever get on a jury panel for a murder case with what happened with your little brother Andy?"

Mary explained that she could not go into all the details, because the judge had told the jurors not to talk to anyone about the case. She mentioned that the trial should be over on Monday, and that she would gladly tell her friend all about it sometime in the next week.

"Janet, I was also calling to ask you for a simple favor," Mary said.

Hesitantly, Janet agreed. "What do you need me to do?"

Mary said, "Bless your heart because I need a good friend today who will ask me what I need, instead of questioning me about what I am doing." Mary explained to Janet that she and Ricky were having a rough week in their relationship, mainly because she was unable to share with him what she was experiencing at the courthouse. Mary said, "I want you and your family to sit with us at church on Sunday. You can be a buffer, if you will, between Ricky and me. I'm hoping that you will be able to eliminate some of the tension that we are feeling between us, just by sitting with us.

"On Monday, the trial should be over, and the tension should be eliminated once I am able to share the details of the trial with Ricky. So please say yes, and let's meet 45 minutes before the service begins close to the front by the main stage. You can sit next to me. Will you do that for me?"

"Of course," Janet replied, "if you'll meet me for dinner next week so we can really talk." Janet knew there was much more to be learned from her friend, and she prayed that God would guide Mary to make the right decisions regarding the tension in her marriage.

On Saturday, Mary was happy to spend some time with her children. To Mary, Bobby and Cary provided a glorious light to the areas of her life that were feeling a little dark at the moment. She felt grateful for their energy and the pureness that resided in their hearts. Mary absorbed their love, feeling blessed that they were a part of her life.

Ricky and Mary arrived at church early that Sunday morning, and met up with Janet and her husband. Ricky, too, was relieved that he would have another man of God to speak with for a little while before the service started. He could not remember the last time he had felt so awkward around his wife, and he certainly didn't like the burning feeling that was in his stomach.

The music began, and they all took their seats, with Janet sitting next to Mary as promised. Mary reached for Janet's hand, and Janet took it in both of hers, giving her friend comfort and strength. Janet also said a quick prayer, asking God to help the pastor say something that would help Mary and Ricky with the tension in their relationship.

The pastor started by saying, "In the beginning, God only gave us one warning or one rule to follow. He gave Adam and Eve the rule because he knew that they were capable of being deceived. In Genesis 2:16, we read, '*But the Lord God warned him, You may freely eat the fruit of every tree in the garden,* 17 *except the tree of the knowledge of good and evil. If you eat its fruit, you are sure to die.*' Make sure you don't gloss over what God is telling us here. God is telling us there is good and evil. He is telling us that both existed before Adam and Eve sinned, and both exist in this world we live in today."

Eyes on the congregation, the pastor continued, "In the beginning Satan took the role of the serpent, and stroked Eve's selfish desires by telling her she could be just like God if she would partake of the tree of the knowledge of good and evil. Genesis 3:4 reads, '*You won't die the serpent replied to the woman.* Verse 5, *God knows that your eyes will be opened as soon as you eat it, and you will be like God, knowing both good and evil.*'

"God wants us to be close to him and follow his ways because he knows that we are very capable of being deceived. God knows that we are very capable of deceiving others if we allow and act upon the temptations that Satan shrewdly puts in front of our minds and our hearts.

Look at Genesis 3:13, '*Then the Lord God asked the woman, What have you done? The serpent deceived me, she replied.*'"

The pastor paused. "I'm going to ask you a series of questions today, and I want you to discuss them with your families later today and over the next few weeks. What is Satan really after? The other tree in the Garden of Eden was the tree of life, which is symbolic of having eternal life with God through his son, Jesus Christ. God gave us the choice to follow him or to follow the serpent. Satan desires to lure as many followers and souls away from God because he wants to be God and rule over mankind. Like Eve, many of us today choose, by making lifestyle decisions, to be lured away from God.

"Could it be that there are many who walk among us who desire to be like God or worship someone or something other than God Almighty, our Creator? Is this partially the reason why we experience so many negative things that occur within our families, our communities, our schools, and our governments?

"I ask these questions because I believe I already know the answers. I want our congregation, our nation, and the world to start thinking about where we place God in our lives. In a world obsessed with selfies and narcissism, do we really believe we are following God, or are we following the deceiver? Are we deceiving ourselves and others by claiming to be Christians?

"Revelation 12:9 tells us, '*This great dragon—the ancient serpent called the devil, or Satan, the one deceiving the whole world—was thrown down to the earth with all his angels.*' It is also written that we shall have many false prophets who say they are followers of Jesus Christ, but their actions do not follow their words and deeds."

The pastor paused for a few moments as he picked up a different Bible from his pulpit and continued, "As I was referencing the New International Version Life Application Study Bible, I found a definition of hypocrisy that I would like to share with you. Hypocrisy is pretending to be something you are not and have no intention of being.

"Jesus called the Pharisees hypocrites because they worshiped God for the wrong reasons. Their worship was not motivated by love, but by a desire to attain profit, to appear holy, and to increase their status within their community. We become hypocrites when we (1) pay more attention to reputation then to character, (2) carefully follow certain religious practices while allowing our hearts to remain distant from God, and (3) emphasize our virtues, but others' sins.

"Being a pastor for so many years, I have met many people who I believe deep down are counterfeit Christians. In part, counterfeit Christians do not verbally deny that Jesus Christ came in a real body and walked this earth. They don't deny that the Father and the Holy Spirit exist. But counterfeit Christians do not follow the teachings of Jesus Christ closely. Their knowledge is limited, and they can easily be deceived by the devil or be a deceiver for Satan, knowingly or unknowingly.

"Eve admitted she was deceived by the serpent. What did Eve do after being deceived by the serpent and partaking of the fruit? Eve became the deceiver as she offered the forbidden fruit to her husband, Adam. When we knowingly or unknowing become the deceiver, we take our brothers and sisters away from their walk toward God, and our relationship with our creator diminishes.

"Counterfeit Christians also have the ability to talk a good game, show up for church every Sunday and speak a beautiful prayer, just to be heard or to receive an accolade. But when the doors close, and no one is around to hear the words that come from their hearts and to see the actions their mind has commanded, they are far from walking in the footsteps of Jesus Christ, similar to a hypocrite as defined earlier.

"Be careful of the dangers of counterfeit Christianity in your family, in the organizations you support, and the political candidates you vote for. Satan and his offspring are relentless in their battle against God's children, the true Christians who are actively living by the truth of Jesus Christ and the word of God.

"Please turn your Bibles to the great book of John, chapter 8 verse 47, which reads, '*Anyone who belongs to God listens gladly to the words of God. But you don't listen because you do not belong to God.'* If you do not belong to God as it is quoted in John 8:47, what is the alternative? Who do you belong to? Satan? Didn't Jesus warn us that there would be an Antichrist?

"The Antichrist is someone who wants to appear to be holy and pretends to be the Son of God, Jesus Christ. In other words, the Antichrist will lead all the counterfeit Christians away from Jesus Christ." He paused again. "For your information, I have already told the staff to be prepared to receive a higher amount of phone calls and emails regarding today's message."

There were some chuckles from the congregation, and the pastor continued. "Jesus Christ explains how some of us become members of the counterfeit Christian culture. Please turn your Bibles to Matthew 13 where we will cover verses 3-9. *'Listen! A farmer went out to plant some seeds. As he scattered them across his field, some seeds fell on a footpath, and the birds came and ate them.*

"'Other seeds fell on shallow soil with underlying rock. The seeds sprouted quickly because the soil was shallow. But the plants soon wilted under the hot sun, and since they didn't have deep roots, they died. Other seeds fell among thorns that grew up and choked the tender plants. Still other seeds fell on fertile soil, and they produced a crop that was thirty, sixty and even a hundred times as much as had been planted! Anyone with ears to hear should listen and understand.'"

The pastor said, "Listen closely. The seed is consistent because it is God's Word, that is to say God's plan and purpose for your life that He has given you. The four different types of soil defined in this parable reflect the condition of your heart, your mind, and your soul. Jesus explains the parable about the farmer planting seeds in the book of Matthew.

"Matthew 13: 19-23: *'The seed that fell on the footpath represents those who hear the message about the Kingdom and don't understand it. Then the evil one comes and snatches away the seed that was planted in their hearts. The seed on the rocky soil represents those who hear the*

*message and immediately receive it with joy. But since they don't have
deep roots, they don't last long. They fall away as soon as they have
problems or are persecuted for believing God's word.*

*"'The seed that fell among the thorns represents those who hear
God's word, but all too quickly the message is crowded out by the wor-
ries of this life and the lure of wealth, so no fruit is produced. The seed
that fell on good soil represents those who truly hear and understand
God's word and produce a harvest of thirty, sixty, or even a hundred
times as much as had been planted!'"*

The pastor looked out at the congregation. "The warning here: Do
not let your heart be choked out before it can be developed and allowed
to produce fruit for God. Do not allow your life to be so cluttered that
you have no time to pray or read the love letter, the Bible, which was
sent to you by God. Keep your focus on God so He can provide daily
nourishment to your soul.

"Listen closely, because where you spend eternity is what is being discussed in these verses. If you noticed in the parable we just reviewed, there are four types of soils and four types of people who live
in this world. Please notice that only one of the four types is considered
to be good by Jesus Christ, so what happens to the souls of the other
three types of people? Let's continue in the book of Matthew by reading chapter 13: verses 24-30:

"'*The Kingdom of Heaven is like a farmer who planted good seed
in his field. But that night as the workers slept, his enemy came and
planted weeds among the wheat, then slipped away. When the crop
began to grow and produce grain, the weeds also grew. The farmer's
workers went to him and said, Sir, the field where you planted that good
seed is full of weeds! Where did they come from? An enemy did this,
the farmer exclaimed. Should we pull out the weeds? No, he replied,
you'll uproot the wheat if you do. Let both grow together until the harvest. Then I will tell the harvesters to sort out the weeds, tie them into
bundles, and burn them, and to put the wheat in the barn.'*"

The pastor lowered his voice. "Read and understand, because

through faith, every true Christian can receive eternal life and can never perish. But beware that the enemy sower, which is to say Satan himself, will masquerade as an angel of light, and if you do not understand God's word, Satan may steal your soul.

"One day, God himself will judge us, and He alone will determine if you're placed in the bundle that is burned. Or, God can decide if you will be placed in the barn and experience eternity with God who loves us dearly. It is the condition of your mind and heart that will determine what God's judgment will be for you. Only a fraction will receive the gospel of Jesus Christ, and in knowing thyself, will you be one of them?

"Please turn to Proverbs Chapter 6:16. It is intentional that I have been asking you to look up scripture in the Old Testament as well as the New Testament this morning. Proverbs 6:16-19 reads, *'There are six things the Lord hates – no, seven things he detests: haughty eyes, a lying tongue, hands that kill the innocent, a heart that plots evil, feet that race to do wrong, a false witness who pours out lies, a person who sows discord in a family.'*

"Folks, you can tell these are not my words that I am sharing with you this morning; these are words from God that have been written and preserved for you, his children. The Bible was created for you so that you may learn and understand who God is. God wants you to know what He has done for you in the past, what He is doing for you in the present, and what He has planned for you in His future. It is all here in black and white, written to you and for you with much love.

"Now turn to 1 Samuel 10:9: *'As Saul turned and started to leave, God gave him a new heart, and all Samuel's signs were fulfilled that day.'* This verse speaks to the time when Saul was anointed the first man king of the nation of Israel. I share this verse with you to remind you that if your heart condition is not currently adequate to follow the commands of Jesus Christ, God can provide you with a new heart. Just pray and ask him for his guidance and his assistance. All things are possible for God.

"Okay, we're in the bottom of the ninth inning. Please turn to the last book in the Bible, Revelation Chapter 20:12-15: '*I saw the dead, both great and small, standing before God's throne. And the books were opened, including the Book of Life. And the dead were judged according to what they had done, as recorded in the books. The sea gave up its dead, and death and the grave gave up their dead. And all were judged according to their deeds. Then death and the grave were thrown into the lake of fire. This lake of fire is the second death. And anyone whose name was not found recorded in the Book of Life was thrown into the lake of fire.'*

"Folks, please note that verse 13 states that all are judged according to their deeds or according to their works. This means that on Judgment Day, God will open His books and He will reveal to you and me what we truthfully did with our time here on Earth. How did we treat His children? Were we deceived by the evil one, and did we ever repent for our sins that we committed?

"Revelation 14:13 says**,** '*And I heard a voice from heaven saying, write this down: Blessed are those who die in the Lord from now on. Yes, says the Spirit, they are blessed indeed, for they will rest from their hard work; for their good deeds follow them!'*

"I bring these passages to your attention because from today going forward, I want you to live your life knowing that what you do here on Earth will be judged by God Himself. I beg of you that you start treating all of God's children better and take the time to read the letter that God Himself has left behind for you. Everything you need to manage your life, to give wisdom to your children, everything you need is right here in this Bible.

"Use the golden rule to set your standard on how to treat people at work, at the grocery store, in the library, on the street, in your car, and in your church. Matthew 7:12 says, '*Do to others whatever you would like them to do to you. This is the essence of all that is taught in the law and the prophets.*' Jesus told us in John 13: 34-35, '*So now I am giving you a new commandment: Love each other. Just as I have loved you,*

you should love each other. Your love for one another will prove to the world that you are my disciples.'

"Let's close with a prayer. Heavenly Father, Creator of all that is seen and unseen, we thank you for your son, Jesus Christ, who sacrificed His life for our sins. We ask you for your love, and we ask you to help us understand your word so that we can better serve you with the lives you have given us. Lift us up and protect our hearts so that we may live day to day with clean hands and a pure heart that brings you glory.

"We understand that one day we will see you face to face. I ask you to take every one of us in this room today and place us in your barn, your kingdom. There, we will bask in your love and in your glory, forever and forever. Please Father God, I ask you to protect your flock from the temptations of this world, and more specifically, the temptations of the devil. I pray for this in your precious son's name, our Lord and Savior, Jesus Christ! Amen."

"Wow," was the first word from Janet's mouth to her family as well as to Mary. Since they had looked up so many Bible verses throughout the sermon, they were no longer holding hands. Although Janet had prayed for God to use the pastor to help Mary and Ricky's relationship, she had never dreamed the pastor would talk about being a hypocrite and a counterfeit Christian, bundles being burned, or the wheat being placed in the barn.

"Wow," Janet said a second time. She turned to Mary and told her she had to leave with her family because she wanted to review the way they had been living, and the way they had been treating others.

Mary felt dazed. She heard Janet speaking, and she saw her leave her seat, but she could not bring herself to get up. After what seemed a very long time, Mary realized Ricky was standing in front of her, asking if she was ready to go home. Ricky said, "Janet already left with her family, and the kids are getting restless, so we should get going."

Mary heard Ricky, but she felt paralyzed, trapped in a body that could not move a muscle. Finally, Ricky reached down and took Mary's hand, snapping her out of her paralysis. It was the first time Ricky had touched her in nearly a week!

Mary looked up into Ricky's eyes and began to sob. Cary immediately leaned against her, anxiously crying, "What's wrong, Mommy, what's wrong?" Ricky pulled Mary out of her seat and hugged her tightly.

The tears were rolling down Mary's cheeks, and Ricky's eyes were welling up as well. Mary whispered in Ricky's ear, "I miss you." Unaccustomed to their parents' tears, Bobby and Cary also began to cry and hug their parents. None of them really knowing exactly why they were crying, but they were crying nonetheless. After a few minutes, the family was able to regain its composure and walk toward the parking lot in silence, Mary leaning heavily on Ricky.

Mary's mother, Julie, was outside chatting with friends. As Mary and Ricky approached, she made a comment about the thought-provoking sermon the pastor had prepared for them that day. "I am on my way to have lunch with my girlfriends, but let's catch up later and talk about what was discussed here today at church," she said. "I really want to know what kind of lifestyle choices we are making, and what you think about what was said by the pastor." Looking more closely at her daughter, Julie could tell Mary had been crying. "Mary, are you okay?"

Mary managed to say, "Yes, Mom. Let's catch up later. If not this evening, let's talk on Monday."

Julie agreed, adding, "I can tell by the tears streaming down your cheeks that today's message has had an impact on your heart. I look forward to speaking with all of you tomorrow."

In silence, Ricky, Mary and the children drove home. Finally, Bobby broke the silence with his usual question. "What's for dinner?"

Still in a daze, Mary said, "Ricky, I have a very bad headache, and I would like to go to bed when we get home. Can you please make dinner for the children?"

Ricky replied that he could.

The drive seemed an eternity to Mary, and once home she escaped to their bedroom, took three aspirin, and lay down on her bed in the fetal position. Although Mary truly did have a headache, she also really did not want to talk about the sermon. She knew that Ricky would want to discuss the pastor's message as he usually did, but that message seemed even more meaningful than usual to Mary, considering what had occurred in the past week with the trial.

It seemed to Mary that the message today was targeting her recent actions and decisions. She clearly had made the decision that she wanted to be involved in the murder trial as a member of the jury panel, even if she had to lie to the people she cared about. Mary felt as though she were standing in a heavy fog, and her mind was confused as she thought about the different paths she could take to find her way home again. She closed her eyes and felt a burden of sadness in her heart, and she began to cry once again.

Lying in the bed, Mary admitted to herself that she had been a hypocrite many times. Just last Sunday, for instance, she had stood with a small group of church friends and talked about a couple that was having marriage problems. She asked herself, "Were we really trying to figure out a way to help them, or were we just gossiping?"

Mary reflected briefly about the seven things that the Lord hates and the fact that she had to face the 11 other jury members in the morning, and then she fell into a deep sleep.

Chapter Thirteen

Final Day of Deliberations

Monday morning arrived, and the jurors were ready to burst with conversation. However, we knew we could not speak about the case until we were led by the bailiff to the jury deliberation room. We were distracted somewhat as we waited because a whole new group of potential jurors had arrived, and they had to be instructed just like we had been one week prior.

The juror instructional video came on again, and several people commented that it must have been the 10th time we had seen it since we were assigned to the case. We felt like veterans at this point, and that thought briefly took away the tension of not knowing what Mary's point of view would be after a weekend away from the courthouse.

Bailiff Adams appeared in the assembly room, and after a few minutes he took us away to our very familiar jury deliberation room. As soon as he left and we had all said our "good mornings," I turned to Mary. "Let's jump right into it," I said. "Mary, I do not want to seem like I am picking on you, but I have to ask if your decision changed over the weekend?"

Mary said, "No, Terry, my decision did not change. I feel the same as I did before we left for the weekend." Again, you could hear a collective gasp from the jury panel at her announcement.

"OK," I said. "Here are three copies of the Charge of the Court, the document that the judge gave us. I want us to break into three groups of four and each group will take a copy. I want you to read along as one of us reads each word, paragraph, and page out loud."

This plan was quickly met with dismay. A juror said, "Terry, there is no point to reading these 11 pages because Mary's mind is made up, and I think it is a waste of our time."

Two other jurors said the same thing. I simply replied, "As foreman of this jury panel, I want to make sure if the judge asks me does everyone understand the definition of the charges, I will be able to tell her, 'Yes, Your Honor.'" The jurors agreed, and I asked for a volunteer to read the document to us.

Marilyn started reading out loud, and by the time she got to the fifth paragraph everyone was excited again. The fifth paragraph stated, "Mr. Paulson is presumed to be innocent until proven guilty. Mr. Paulson enters upon the trial of the case with the presumption of innocence in his favor. This presumption remains with Mr. Paulson until it is overcome by the State with evidence which is sufficient to convince you beyond a reasonable doubt; that Mr. Paulson is guilty of the offense charged.

"No person shall be convicted of any crime unless and until each element of the crime is proven beyond a reasonable doubt. The burden of proof rests upon the State to prove every material allegation of the indictment. And every essential element of the crime charged beyond a reasonable doubt." All of the jurors were sitting on the edge of their seats, biting their tongues.

Marilyn continued, "There is no burden of proof upon Mr. Paulson whatsoever, and the burden never shifts to Mr. Paulson to prove his innocence. When a defense such as self-defense is raised by the evidence, the burden is on the State to negate or disprove it beyond a reasonable doubt."

I could tell the atmosphere in the deliberation room had changed to anticipation; no longer did it seem a waste of time to read the document. The jurors were eager to have more specific dialogue on the law and how it pertained to Paulson's actions that dreadful night. Many wanted to start discussing what they had been hearing and reading, but I asked that we wait until we read the next paragraph.

Marilyn continued, "The State is not required to prove the guilt of the accused beyond all doubt or to a mathematical certainty. A reasonable doubt means just what it says. A reasonable doubt is a doubt of a fair-minded, impartial juror, honestly seeking truth. It is a doubt based upon common sense and reason. It does not mean a vague or arbitrary doubt, but is a doubt for which a reason can be given, arising from a consideration of the evidence, a lack of evidence, a conflict in the evidence, or any combination of these."

After Marilyn finished reading, I opened the table for discussion, asking that we use the raise-your-hand rule so not everyone was talking at once. Marvin was ready to burst, so I called on him to share his thoughts, and he turned directly to Mary. "Do you really think the State of Georgia proved beyond a shadow of a doubt that Paulson intended to kill Candlestick?"

Mary looked at Marvin and asked for a few moments to think about his question. Wanting to verify that she understood his question, she asked Marvin, "Are you asking me if the State of Georgia proved that Paulson wanted to kill Candlestick?"

Marvin said, "Yes, that is exactly my question." The room was deathly quiet. This seemed like another defining moment for all of us on the jury panel.

If Mary said no, then we would all be in agreement that "not guilty" would apply to all charges against Paulson. After pondering at length, Mary replied, "Yes, I do believe that the State proved beyond a reasonable doubt that Paulson wanted to kill Candlestick. Candlestick had just roughed him up and stolen his money, and he wanted to get even with him."

The room was filled with sighs of disbelief, and a few jurors even spun around in their chairs, mumbling under their breaths. Shelby jumped into the conversation without waiting to be called. "Mary, regarding the last paragraph we just read, do you think a fair-minded, impartial juror, honestly seeking the truth, would say that self-defense was eliminated as an option by the State's prosecuting attorney?"

Mary did not reply to this question immediately. Shelby had made a great point, and others wanted to jump in and say something, too, but I said, "Let's wait a minute or two to give Mary time to answer Shelby's question."

After several minutes of complete silence, it became obvious that Mary was not going to answer the question. Her silence made no sense to the rest of us, who could not figure out how the state's attorney had proved beyond a reasonable doubt that self-defense was impossible.

I asked Mary, "Since you are not going to answer that question, can you tell me what specifically the prosecutor did or said during the trial that made you believe that self-defense is not an option or a possibility? Perhaps the rest of us in this room missed something, and you can enlighten us." Again, Mary did not speak, and the rest of the group waited in silent frustration.

Just as I was going to suggest we keep reading the document, Anne raised her voice to Mary, "I cannot believe you are not answering these questions. I cannot believe that you truly believe that the lawyer for the State of Georgia proved beyond a reasonable doubt that self-defense is not applicable in this case. On Friday of last week, Mary, I was sitting in this room, and Terry was at the board writing down what we agreed about in this case.

"You said you believed Paulson was afraid for his life in the back seat. Everyone in this room heard you say you believed he was afraid for his life. We all heard you and saw you change your decision when you realized Paulson was going to be found not guilty. You changed your mind, Mary. Everyone was here. So what are you doing?"

Mary stared back at Anne with a combination of hatred and disbelief in her eyes. The rest of us in the room were stunned at Anne's outburst, but we certainly couldn't argue with her sentiment. The room went silent once again. Although Anne had spoken the truth, I did not believe that continuing the conversation would have any benefit. Mary was not going to reverse her opinion to match the other 11 jurors in the room.

After about five more minutes of silence waiting on Mary to respond, I finally said, "Let's continue reading the document." Once again several members of the jury asked why. Since we were not going to have a unanimous vote, we might as well stop and call in the bailiff. I said, "I understand your feelings of helplessness, but we are going to continue to finish reading this document, and then we will do a formal vote on all the charges."

The reading continued, pausing only after Marilyn read about the judge discussing our responsibility as a juror. The judge noted that it was our responsibility to determine the facts of the case from all the evidence presented. Then we had to apply the law she explained to us to the facts as we determined them.

Marilyn had paused in her reading, but no one had the energy left to continue the debate. We were like the fish hooked on a reel. It starts with a fight but is slowly worn down until there is no fight left in it. Mary had worn us down, and we did not have much fight left in us. We knew a person's future was at stake, but our ability to stand up and fight for him was waning.

Marilyn continued to read, and after several more pages had been read, Anne interrupted again and said, "Mary, I am sorry for losing my temper with you. Even though I do not agree with what you are doing and your opinion of this case, I should have not raised my voice to you, and for that I am sorry."

Mary accepted her apology with a simple, "It's okay."

At that moment, I took control of the conversation and said, "Mary wasn't that awfully nice of Anne to apologize 10 minutes after she yelled at you?"

Mary again just simply said, "Yes," and nodded in agreement.

I asked, "Anne, why did you wait over 10 minutes to apologize to Mary?"

Anne replied, "I needed that time to settle down and regain my composure." Everyone again perked up a little as they began to see where I was taking this discussion.

My focus went back to Mary, and I said, "Mary, it took Anne a little over 10 minutes to settle down after she blurted out her feelings toward you. It took that long for her heart beat to drop back down to normal and for her mind to hear the voice of reason so that she could get out an apology to you."

I paused and then said, "Anne is not in the parking lot at night in the back seat of a car with virtual strangers and $2,000 in her pocket. Anne did not have a gun pointed at her face, and it still took her 10 minutes to regain her composure."

I continued with my line of questioning by asking Mary, "Do you really think it is not possible that Paulson needed a lot more time than taking two or three steps out of the car for his heartbeat to get back to normal? And to let the adrenalin leave his thought processes, and for the voice of reason to take over once again?"

Mary replied, "No, some people can change quicker than others, and I believe Paulson changed that quickly."

Just moments before, as I began the new dialogue, the atmosphere in the deliberation room was like everyone blowing air into a balloon. With every breath exhaled into the balloon, it became bigger and bigger. It was encouraging to feel the balloon getting larger and potentially sail away with the truth on board. Then all of a sudden, Mary gave her defiant reply, and the atmosphere changed like a person who loses his or her grip on the stem of the balloon. Suddenly all the air releases, and the balloon becomes flat once again in matter of seconds.

Deflated, we went back to reading the document for another 40 minutes. I asked the jurors if they had any questions about the charges and definition of the charges, and they said they did not. I thanked Marilyn for reading the document, and I said, "Then let's take our formal vote on the charges."

Count 1 - Murder: 12 not guilty

Lesser included offense of Voluntary Manslaughter: 11 not guilty and 1 guilty

Count 2 - Felony Murder: 12 not guilty

Lesser included offense of Voluntary Manslaughter: 11 not guilty and 1 guilty

Count 3 – Aggravated Assault: 12 not guilty

Count 4 – Possession of Firearm: 11 not guilty and 1 guilty

Count 5 – Possession of Firearm: 11 not guilty and 1 guilty

Count 6 – Possession of Firearm: 12 not guilty

I said to the jury panel, "This is where we currently stand in regards to our vote." Most of the jury panel was visibly upset.

Rosemary said loudly, "That's it, we have a hung jury, and Paulson is going back to jail because of one person in this room. It is not right, it is not justice, and it is morally wrong."

I asked, "Does everyone pretty much agree with that statement? Is that what you feel is happening here in this room?" Everyone except Mary nodded in agreement. I asked the jury panel if they agreed with Anne when she said we all witnessed Mary changing her mind, and her verdict, while I was at the whiteboard.

"Does everyone agree that Mary had a strong desire for Paulson to be guilty of the offense of voluntary manslaughter? Does everyone remember that Mary said, 'someone died, and someone has to pay'?" Everyone except Mary agreed that the answer to both questions was yes.

I continued, "I anticipated Mary was not going to change her position over the weekend, so in preparation, I have written a two-page letter to the judge. I would like to read it to you, and if you all agree with the contents of this letter, I would like to submit it to the judge from all of us. I am not sure what will happen after the judge reads this letter, but I feel compelled to do something about the injustice that is happening here today."

Mary saw the two pages, swung her chair back around to face the table, got out a piece of paper, and picked up her pen. I started to read the letter, and Mary immediately said she disagreed with what I was reading. I said, "That's okay and expected, but I am looking for the other 10 jurors to give me their feedback on whether or not they believe everything I have written is truthful."

Mary said, "Fine, then I will write my own letter to the judge," and she quickly disengaged once again.

I finished reading the document and everyone verbally agreed that what was written was accurate. We all agreed that it should be submitted so that we could receive some input from Judge Worthington on how to proceed with the deliberations. I also hand wrote a note asking a question on how to complete the verdict form. I looked up and noticed Mary had given up on writing her own document to the judge. I then paged the bailiff and gave him the two-page document and my note so that he could personally take them to Judge Worthington.

During the 30 minutes before the bailiff returned to our room, there was very little conversation among the jury panel. Everyone was truly exhausted. One of the women had a crossword puzzle book in her purse and about six of us asked if we could have a page. We were very grateful to her because the puzzle gave us the opportunity to divert our thoughts and talk about something besides the case.

There was a knock on the door, and the bailiff appeared. He asked Mary to follow him, and we assumed that she was going to have to speak with the judge directly. After a few short minutes, the bailiff entered the room and asked the rest of us to follow him into the courtroom. We all glanced at each other in anticipation of what the judge was going to do or ask of us.

When we sat down in the jury box, Judge Worthington calmly said, "Good afternoon, ladies and gentlemen. A couple of things we need to discuss. I have been going over your notes with the parties and their attorneys while you were not present. First of all, if you'll recall, each count of the indictment as I instructed you does stand separately and on its own.

"We do ask the jurors to consider each case on its own merit and return a verdict as to each count separately. That is why we provide a verdict form that has verdicts as to each count. So there is no requirement that your verdict is identical as to each count, but it can be, of course. So that's an answer to one of your questions.

"In regards to the second note, let me tell you one last thing. Obviously all of you started considering this case last Friday. I think we had given all the evidence and the charge to you around lunchtime on Friday. You indicated you were ready to go home for dinner around 5:30 or 6 Friday night.

"You have come back this Monday morning, and now it is about 4 o'clock in the afternoon. That's a considerable period of time, but obviously the evidence stretched over two or three days, so I don't think it's an undue amount of time. I am going to give you one last charge about the desirability of agreement, if possible.

"The case was carefully and exhaustively tried by both sides. It has been submitted to you for decision and a verdict. I did instruct you about the law, and you do have those documents in the deliberation room for your review. It is the law that a unanimous verdict is required. The verdict must be the conclusion of each juror and not a mere acquiescence in order to reach an agreement.

"I'm going to ask that you consider this case one more time. Listen to the arguments of the other jurors with a disposition to be convinced by them. If you differ in your opinion of the evidence, that difference of opinion should cause all of you to scrutinize the evidence even more closely and then reexamine the grounds for your opinion. Your duty is to decide the issues that have been submitted to you, if you can conscientiously do so.

"As you confer with one another, lay aside all pride of opinion. Bear in mind, the jury room is no place for taking up and maintaining a side simply in the spirit of controversy. Also bear in mind that as jurors, you should not be advocates for either side.

"Determine the truth as it appears from the evidence that was presented to you, and examine the evidence in light of the law within the instructions that I gave you. You, of course, are the sole arbiters of the evidence in this case and you are the sole judges of the law. You are to apply the law in a fashion that was given to you by this Honorable Court.

"So I'm sending you back to retire one more time to examine everything and consider one another's opinion one last time. Thank you. Please follow the bailiff back to the deliberation room."

When we reached the deliberation room, we sat down quietly. I asked God for guidance on what to say or to do; I felt completely helpless. One of the members pulled me aside and said, "I have an international flight tomorrow, and if we do not come to a conclusion soon, I will request to speak with the judge and ask her to relieve me."

Another person said that she could not stay late tonight because she left her medicines at home, and they were crucial to keeping her healthy. Yet another jury member told me in confidence that she was enduring a financial hardship, and if deliberations went into another day, she would request to speak with the judge and ask to be released.

The panel was close to unraveling, and I knew we had to come to a quick decision one way or another. I asked openly if anyone had any ideas on how to proceed as the judge had ordered us to do. The only feedback I received was that several members expressed that there was no hope and that we were truly deadlocked. I asked Mary if there was anything the judge had said to us that would change her answer. She simply replied "No" while looking down at the floor.

I asked Mary if she would explain to us why we should change our verdicts to match hers, for the judge had just told us to consider everyone's opinion. Mary replied that her previous answer was sufficient. I asked her to reiterate it once again for our benefit, and she responded by saying, "Paulson should not have stopped to fire his gun. He should have just kept running."

Two of the other members joined the conversation and started asking Mary questions, but she swiveled her chair and turned her back to the rest of us. We sat for about 10 minutes in complete silence before I said, "It looks like we have to admit that we are in a deadlock, and the result will be a hung jury."

One of the male members was visibly upset, speaking about the oath he had taken the week before in the jury box. He noted that his heart was filled with sadness, and he believed his oath was not being fulfilled by calling it quits. Several others chimed in and expressed the same feelings. One man said that he would have to deal for the rest of his life with the fact that a person he believed should have been acquitted had to go back to jail.

I picked up the official verdict form and started to fill it out. Since we had already taken a formal vote, there was no reason to do it again.

"For the charges that all 12 of us agreed on, I simply placed an "X" by the "not guilty" option on the verdict form. For the charges that Mary voted "guilty" on, I did not place an "X" next to the "guilty" or "not guilty" options. Instead, I wrote "11 not guilty and 1 guilty." I signed the document, called the bailiff and handed him the verdict form.

About five minutes later, the bailiff came back and escorted us to the courtroom. I questioned myself as I walked. Was there anything else I could have done or anything else I could have said to help change Mary's point of view? The answer that kept coming back to me is what Mary had said previously, "Someone died and someone has to pay." With that thought prevailing in her mind, how could she ever be persuaded to seek the truth as we knew it to be?

Chapter Fourteen

The Verdict

Before reviewing the actual verdict form, I am going to tell you about some interesting facts that I found through my research after the trial had ended. First, the previous trial occurred several years before I sat in the jury panel box. The defendant was found guilty of murder and felony murder after the jury deliberated for about two hours. The defendant was later sentenced to life in prison plus five years. The additional five-year prison term was added to life in prison for firing a gun during the commission of a felony.

I also learned that three years before the shooting, McDonald had been involved in an armed robbery. Once again, he was the driver. One afternoon, his passenger got out of his vehicle with a gun and robbed two different places. McDonald and his passenger were arrested, and the money and gun were found when the officers searched their vehicle.

The passenger was convicted of a lesser charge, and he told the police that McDonald was never involved in his robbery plans. Although indicted for armed robbery, McDonald was nol-prossed. *Nolle pros* is Latin for "We shall no longer prosecute," so McDonald was officially off the hook in regards to that armed robbery charge.

I also learned that in the Paulson case, the State of Georgia actually tried on three separate occasions to plea bargain with the defendant and his attorney. The first proposal – for 20 years in jail – actually took place before the trial began. Paulson declined the offer through his attorney.

On Monday evening, just hours before we handed in the verdict, I wrote a note to the judge stating my concern that juror six was no longer following her sworn oath in jury deliberations. That note was read in the courtroom by the judge in the presence of the prosecutor, the defendant, and his attorney. After the judge read the note, a short conference took place in the judge's chamber, and the State made another offer to the defendant.

Prosecutor Albert said, "Your Honor, I have spoken with the chief assistant district attorney in my office, and he has authorized me to make an offer to defense attorney Edwin, a capped recommendation of 15 years, to serve the first 10 in confinement. The defendant would be guaranteed to getting no more than 10 years to serve, plus he would get credit for the years he has served already." Judge Worthington asked, "And that's a plea of guilty to voluntary manslaughter?"

Albert replied, "To voluntary manslaughter, yes, ma'am."

Edwin informed the judge and the prosecutor that although Paulson appreciated the efforts of the prosecutor, "My client does not accept the offer at this time, but he understands that the offer is getting better. Before the trial it was a 20-year offer."

The third attempt from the State to plea bargain with the defendant occurred after I already had signed the verdict form and handed it over to the bailiff. After the judge read it out loud in the presence of the prosecutor, the defendant, and his attorney, the State asked the judge for a two-minute break. During this break, the State offered defense attorney Edwin an eight-year prison term for his client.

Edwin responded, "Your Honor, the district attorney has come down, just for the Court's edification, from the 15-year term capped at 10 years, now down to an eight-year term. Paulson, especially after hearing the verdict, is not going to accept his offer." As soon as Edwin communicated his client's refusal, prosecutor Albert told the judge that he would like to formally withdraw the offer.

The jury panel was then escorted back into the courtroom, where the judge addressed us. "I have received your verdict form, and I'm trying to inquire as to whether or not you in fact reached a verdict, a unanimous verdict, as recorded on this verdict form.

"So I'm going to read this form out loud and publish it in open court. And as I go through each count and publish the verdict, I'm going to ask each member of the jury if that is his or her verdict that was reached, and so we'll do that now.

"We the jury, find Mr. Paulson as to Count 1 murder and there is an X beside not guilty. Let me start with the jury foreman, and I'll have you state your name. I want you to answer the question, is that verdict that was just published, is that the verdict that you freely and voluntarily agreed to in the jury deliberation room?"

I was the first to answer, and then each juror in turn replied. "My name is Terry Rathmann, and that is the verdict that I agreed to."

"Judy Mann. That is the verdict I agreed to."

"Anne Dikhouphiphet. That's the verdict I agreed to."

"Marilyn Schneider. That's the verdict I agreed to."

"Marvin Goodson and I agree with that verdict."

"Ron Frost and I agree with that verdict."

"Steve Christopher and I agree with that verdict."

"Sam Nichols and I agree with that verdict."

When the judge got to Mary, she said, "I have a question. Are you also going to go to the lesser charge? Are you going to say that, too, or do you not?"

The judge responded, "There is a finding marked on Count 1 of murder of not guilty, and I'm just trying to determine if that is the verdict of the Court. Do you have an answer to that?"

Mary replied, "Mary Davis and I voted not guilty on murder."

The jurors continued. "Sang Martinez and I agree to it."

"Rosemary Bonine and I agree to that verdict."

"Shelby Clinton and I agree."

The judge repeated the same verbal vote clarification in open court by asking all 12 members of the panel on every charge to validate the official verdict form that I handed to the bailiff. One by one, each member verbally agreed to his or her specific vote for each individual charge against Paulson. The judge asked about the voluntary manslaughter charge as well, where the form showed the handwritten verdict, which was 11 not guilty, and one guilty. This process took about 10 minutes, and then the judge once again addressed the panel, the attorneys, and the defendant.

"All right. The form is dated, and it's signed by Terry Rathmann as the jury foreperson. That verdict has now been published in open court. Does the State have any additional questions you want me to ask the jury?"

Prosecutor Albert said, "Judge, I've got some issues that I think probably are best if we don't take them up in front of the jurors. There are procedural issues, procedural issues caused by the way they have completed the verdict form, and I'd ask they not be excused yet."

The judge said, "Okay. Members of the jury, I'm going to need you for a few moments more. Let me see if I can resolve this. Please go with the bailiff into the jury deliberation room for a few minutes."

Just as I thought our job was over, we were marched back to the jury deliberation room. When we arrived, we did not speak much, and most of us went back to filling out our crossword puzzles. Twenty long minutes later, the bailiff came to the room and escorted us back to the courtroom.

After we were seated, Judge Worthington again addressed us. "Ladies and gentlemen of the jury, it appears that your duties and deliberations in the case have ended. I am going to go ahead and excuse you all. I would like to thank you very much for your time, your attention, and your hard work in this case.

"If you would like to speak to either attorney at this point you are allowed to do so, but you are under no obligation to do so. Sometimes the attorneys might want to talk with you to get your perspective on what piece of evidence or view point persuaded you to think one way or another. You are released, and thank you once again for your service."

We were taken back to the deliberation room one last time by the bailiff to get our personal items. In a way, I wanted to celebrate that we no longer had to show up at the courthouse each morning, but the instinct to rejoice was dampened by the sadness that I felt because I knew the defendant had to go back to jail that evening.

As we walked out of the secure area into the front of the courtroom door, we met Paulson's mother. She thanked us for our time and the way we voted. She was very sincere as she spoke to five of us who had chosen not to leave immediately.

The prosecutor came up to me and asked what he could have done differently in the trial. He also wanted to know what was discussed in the deliberation room that led to our decision. "You had a tough case to prove," I replied. "If the defendant would have turned around and shot all his rounds into the car, then we might have thought he was seeking revenge. Instead, we felt he was in self-preservation mode." Our conversation only lasted a minute or two, and then the prosecutor left the area.

Edwin, the defense attorney, asked me if he could call me later that week. It turned out that because of the way I filled out the verdict form, the judge and both attorneys had to do some research to determine what charges could be dropped and what charges potentially would need to be reviewed again in a third trial.

Edwin asked if it was possible for me to attend the next court proceeding. He mentioned that I might be called to the stand as a witness to review the jury panel's verdict if need be. I told him I would love to attend the next court proceeding.

On the next two pages you will see a copy of the signed verdict form that was published in open court.

Terry Allen Rathman

IN THE SUPERIOR COURT OF GWINNETT COUNTY

STATE OF GEORGIA

STATE OF GEORGIA,   *

    vs.   *   INDICTMENT

        *

Defendant,   *

JURY VERDICT

(CHECK THE APPROPRIATE LINE ACCORDING TO YOUR UNANIMOUS VERDICT)

WE THE JURY FIND THE DEFENDANT AS TO:

N/A

Count 1 - MURDER:

_____ GUILTY OR __X__ NOT GUILTY

OR

LESSER INCLUDED OFFENSE OF VOLUNTARY MANSLAUGHTER

N/A

_____ GUILTY OR __X__ NOT GUILTY   11 - Not Guilty

    1 - Guilty

Count 2: FELONY MURDER:

_____ GUILTY OR __X__ NOT GUILTY

OR

_____ LESSER INCLUDED OFFENSE OF VOLUNTARY MANSLAUGHTER.

_____ GUILTY OR _____ NOT GUILTY   11 - Not Guilty

GO ON TO NEXT PAGE   1 - Guilty

Count 3: <u>AGGRAVATED ASSAULT</u>:

_____ GUILTY OR   _X_ NOT GUILTY

Count 4: <u>POSSESSION OF FIREARM DURING COMMISSION OF A FELONY</u>

_____ GUILTY OR   _____ NOT GUILTY   11- NoT Guilty

1- Guilty

Count 5: <u>POSSESSION OF FIREARM DURING COMMISSION OF A FELONY</u>

11 - NoT guilty

_____ GUILTY OR   _____ NOT GUILTY

1- Guilty

Count 6: <u>POSSESSION OF FIREARM DURING COMMISSION OF A FELONY</u>

_____ GUILTY OR   _X_ NOT GUILTY

This _____ day of .

[signature]

JURY FOREPERSON

The following Monday, I was sitting in a different courtroom. I had been called as a witness in the case I was a juror for just seven days earlier. The same judge called court into session, and both attorneys spoke with her about the verdict form and the procedures they needed to adhere to going forward.

I was intrigued and educated by watching the back and forth of opinions between the judge, the prosecutor, and the defense attorney. I briefly took the stand as a witness to confirm, once again, the final outcome of the vote. After I left the witness stand, I sat down with two other members of our jury panel who also were interested in finding out how the court was going to rule on our completed verdict form.

The judge said, "After much discussion, the court has made a decision on the charges against Darren Paulson. Count 1 murder, not guilty as the jury panel voted. Count 2, felony murder, not guilty as the jury panel voted. Count 3, aggravated assault, not guilty as the jury panel voted. As far as counts 4, 5 and 6, I have decided to drop these three charges because by the time we would have another trial, the statute of limitations would have expired.

"As far as the lesser charge of involuntary manslaughter, I have decided not to drop that charge because the jury panel was deadlocked on this charge. Defense attorney Edwin, you will have to appeal my decision to the Georgia Supreme Court, and they can make a decision on the verdict form in regards to the charge of involuntary manslaughter."

Edwin did just that, filing an appeal with the Georgia Supreme Court, and it took almost three years to plead his case. During those three years the defendant, Darren Paulson, had to stay in jail. In late 2013, the Georgia Supreme Court overturned the trial court's decision. The ruling judge said, "In this case, we hold that the jury in acquitting Paulson of malice murder, felony murder, and aggravated assault necessarily determined that Paulson acted in self-defense and that this issue of ultimate fact constitutes a critical element of voluntary manslaughter. Thus, we conclude that double jeopardy bars the State from prosecuting Paulson again for voluntary manslaughter."

Double jeopardy is prohibited by the United States and the Georgia Constitution. The Georgia Supreme Court ordered the case dismissed, and Darren Paulson was released from jail almost three years after our trial ended.

Chapter Fifteen

Someone Died and Someone Has to Pay

The deliberations were over, and the verdict had been accepted by the judge and published in open court. Mary felt a sense of relief that the trial had concluded, and the outcome that she desired had been fulfilled. She didn't waste any time getting out of the courthouse; she had no desire to speak to any of the juror members, the attorneys, or Paulson's mother.

Once Mary got behind the wheel of her car, a wave of emotion swept over her and she began to cry uncontrollably. Finally, after catching her breath, her thoughts turned to her brother Andy, and she decided to call her mother while driving home to give her the good news about the trial.

Mary gave her mother a quick summary of the trial, telling Julie that she had been the only juror who saw clearly the defendant's guilt. Mary explained to her mom how the other 11 jurors kept trying to persuade her to change her mind, but she stuck to her guns and levied a guilty charge of voluntary manslaughter. She told her mother she wished the people involved with Andy's shooting would have been caught so she could have gone to their trial.

In a celebratory tone, Mary said, "There is one less bad guy on the street tonight who will not be able to take another person's life, because he is staying in jail. Thank God, because the family of the victim can rest easy tonight knowing justice has been served."

This was the first time Mary had spoken with her mother about the trial since it had begun, and Julie had trouble digesting all that her daughter was saying. "Sounds like you have had a busy week," she said. "I'll come over to your house tonight and you can give me all the details of the trial then."

Mary said, "No, not tonight. I have to tell Ricky first. Let's catch up this weekend."

Julie didn't press the issue, and said she would call Mary later to arrange a time they could talk. Mary felt relieved that she had finally been able to tell her mother about what had been going on in her world for the last seven days. If anyone would understand how she felt, it would be Julie.

As Mary pulled into her driveway, she saw that Ricky was already home from work. She was excited to see him and tell him and the kids the good news. The three of them were waiting for her in the kitchen, their hot dogs and macaroni and cheese all ready for dinner. Ricky said, "Hello, you're just in time for dinner."

Bobby quickly asked, "So what happened, Mom? Is the trial over?"

Sitting down at the table, Mary said, "Hang on and let your dad say grace before we eat, and then I will tell you what happened at the courthouse today."

Again, Ricky's prayer was a little different from his normal. "Heavenly Father, I thank you for the food we are about to receive, and I thank you for a healthy family. Tonight, I ask that you touch our hearts and make them pure. Please give us the wisdom to see clearly what you want us to do with the lives you have given us. May all that we do and may all that we say bring you honor. I pray for peace and harmony in your holy son's name, Jesus Christ. Amen."

Mary told the children that tomorrow she would not have to go back to the courthouse because the verdict had been submitted and accepted by the judge. The children began asking questions faster than their mother could possibly reply, so Mary told them to stop speaking and to give her a chance to tell them what had happened. Then, if they had any questions, they could ask her.

Addressing the children, Mary said, "The shooter had a chance to walk away from the car without firing his weapon. He had already had at least one foot out of the car when he pulled the trigger that killed the man in the front passenger seat. If the defendant would have just kept walking or running away, no one would have had to die that night.

"Since the defendant did not go into the car that evening looking to kill someone, he was not guilty of murder. But when the defendant sat in the back seat of the car that night, he knowingly put himself in a situation of high risk. Some speculated the meeting was arranged for a marijuana transaction. So when the defendant killed the man by firing his gun, he was then guilty of voluntary manslaughter.

"So kids, your dad and I don't want you to put yourselves in any high-risk situations. If you are around someone that you know is doing something wrong, just walk away before they get you into trouble or, even worse, get you hurt. Okay?"

Bobby and Cary both nodded in agreement, and Bobby asked, "Is the guy in jail now?"

Mary said, "Yes, the guards took him from the courtroom directly to jail."

Bobby asked, "Can we leave the table so we can call our friends and let them know the defendant went to jail?"

Mary replied, "Yes, you are dismissed," and she finally looked at Ricky.

As he was leaving the table, Bobby said, "Cool, Mom, very cool." Mary watched Bobby running away from the dinner table, pleased to be considered a "cool mom" for once.

Ricky and Mary began clearing the table, and Ricky mentioned that the case sounded very interesting. Mary said, "It really was very interesting, Andy."

Ricky said, "What? Did you just call me Andy?"

Mary shook her head. "I'm sorry, honey. I have been thinking about him a lot lately. I called Mom on the way home, and we talked about Andy briefly. Maybe we can have her over for dinner later this week."

Ricky said, "Sure. But now that the trial is over, you and I are allowed to discuss what you experienced during this past week as the attorneys brought in witnesses and tried their best to persuade you to think one way or another."

Mary said, "Yes, no more restrictions. Ricky, I felt really good about serving and giving back to the community. It was exciting to be a part of this trial. I remember looking at the body language of the defendant, as well as the witnesses. I could tell a lot about the defendant by his body language and by the way he spoke, once he was on the witness stand."

Ricky simply said, "Interesting." Mary continued to give him some other moments in the trial that she found interesting and relevant to what happened that night in the car.

After Mary seemed to be finished, Ricky asked her about the six charges filed against the defendant. Ricky said, "You mentioned at the dinner table to the kids that the defendant was not guilty of murder. So everyone agreed that he was not guilty of murder?"

"Yes, all of us agreed that the defendant did not plan that night to kill the victim, or anyone else for that matter."

Ricky said, "I guess I am assuming that everyone else voted against the other charges as well, but you said he was guilty of manslaughter. I am just curious how the 12 of you worked together to come to that conclusion. Remember that trial about the contract dispute between the two business owners I was involved in three years ago?"

"Yes, I remember," replied Mary.

"Well, the hard part of that case was when all 12 of the jurors were in the room deliberating," Ricky said. "We had a difficult time agreeing with each other regarding the defendant being guilty or innocent. The foreperson did a good job keeping us aligned with what was relevant to the case. So I'm just curious … How or why did you all eventually come to the conclusion that the defendant was guilty of voluntary manslaughter and not the murder charge?"

Mary enthusiastically said, "Well, that is the beauty of it. The other 11 jurors didn't recognize the defendant's guilt, but I did, and that is what got him convicted."

As Mary finished speaking, the doorbell rang, and Ricky got up to answer it. Mary's mother, Julie, was at the door. Ricky said, "Hello, Julie, this is a pleasant surprise."

Mary called out, "Mom, what are you doing here? I thought you were going to call me and get together this weekend."

Julie replied, "Well, based on our phone conversation about the trial, I really wanted to come over tonight and learn more about what you experienced."

Mary responded, "Come on in the kitchen, Mom. I was just telling Andy that the other 11 juror members did not find the defendant guilty of voluntary manslaughter. I agreed with all the juror members that the defendant was not guilty of murder and felony murder. But, I knew he was guilty of the voluntary manslaughter charge."

Julie asked, "Honey, did you just call Ricky, Andy?"

Ricky nodded. "That's the second time tonight she called me Andy. I'm starting to get a little concerned about it."

Mary quickly said she was sorry. "With all the excitement about the trial and me talking to Mom about Andy earlier today, it just slipped out. Sorry, honey, it won't happen again."

The three of them sat down at the kitchen table as Ricky replied, "Okay, but let me make sure I didn't misunderstand you regarding the vote count within the jury panel. So 11 of the jury members voted not guilty concerning the voluntary manslaughter charge, and you were the single vote that deemed the defendant guilty of that charge?"

"Yes, that is how it happened," Mary said. "I saw what the other 11 could not see."

Puzzled, Ricky glanced at Julie and then asked his wife, "What did you see that the other 11 jury members didn't see that made you want to convict the defendant of manslaughter?"

"I saw him sitting in his chair by the defense attorney wearing his new suit and sporting a new haircut. His body language told me a lot about him, and the way he spoke, I could tell he was a thug. But most of all, he had a chance to walk away from that parking lot without pulling the trigger. If he would have just walked away or even run out of that parking lot, then the victim would be alive today. But he pulled the trigger, and someone died, so someone had to pay. And justice has been served."

Glancing at Ricky, Julie turned to Mary. "I have a confession to make," Julie said. "I called Ricky after I got off the phone with you. I told him I was concerned about how you described what happened at the trial and the role or position you took on the jury panel.

"Listening to you tonight, I have to say that I am quite concerned about your perception of what is going on around you. I spoke to Ricky, and he told me that during the *voir dire* process you told the attorneys and the judge that you were frustrated about the police investigation of Andy's death. Is that true?"

Mary said, "Hold on a minute. Why are both of you plotting against me? What I did today was the right thing to do, and the streets are a safer place because of it."

Ricky said, "That may be the case. I love you, but I am scared for you, and I am scared for me, and I am scared for our children."

Defensively, Mary asked, "What do you mean by that?"

"Honey, I am concerned first and foremost about what you said or didn't say to the attorneys that they did not disqualify you from being on this case during the *voir dire* process," Ricky explained. "We briefly talked about that the other night, but our conversation got heated, and I left it alone, knowing that eventually the case would end and we could talk in more depth about the situation. I am regretting now that I didn't continue our conversation that evening in order to find out what truly happened during your dialogue with the attorneys and the judge.

"I am also very concerned that you happened to be the only person out of 12 people who saw that the defendant was guilty of the manslaughter charge. I am troubled that you feel, because of your brilliance, you made the world a safer place because you took down a person you considered a thug. Something very serious has happened this past week that will impact many lives, now and in the future."

As Ricky spoke, Mary's facial expression changed from excitement to frustration to anger. Now, her mother spoke, saying she agreed with Ricky. "Something terrible has happened, and I am not quite sure what it is yet, but my spirit can sense it," Julie said. "When you called me on the phone, you sounded like you had just caught Andy's killer single handedly. Then I find out tonight that you have called your husband Andy two times.

"I have forgiven the unknown people who were responsible for your brother's death. I have forgiven them, and because of that forgiveness, I have peace in my heart and my life. Mary, I thought you did the same years ago.

"I know for the first two years after his death that you were quite involved with the investigation, perhaps too involved. I didn't object, and I let you follow your instinct because you were an adult who was married, and about to have her own child. Now, I hear the way you talk about this trial as if you received some type of redemption for all those years that have gone by without knowing the people who killed your brother. Honey, what is happening to you?"

After a long pause, Mary said, "I don't know, Mom," and then she started to sob uncontrollably. Both Ricky and Julie sat by her side, holding her hands and asking her to let it all out. They begged her to release the truth, and to release whatever burden her heart was carrying.

Finally, Mary was able to speak. "I will tell you the truth, but please don't judge me. Please do not condemn me for what I have done. I would not be able to bear it if you both stopped loving me for what I have done this past week."

Both Ricky and Julie looked at each other and promised Mary that they would continue to love her no matter what she had done.

Mary regained some composure and was able to speak and be heard through her tears. "When I received the summons in the mail, I was excited, and I really wanted to be part of an important case," she said. "I didn't imagine at the time that I would be presented with the opportunity to be on a murder trial, but I found myself hoping and wishing for the chance to be assigned to a very important case.

"Then, that morning, the judge said they were selecting a jury panel because the defendant shot a man with his pistol, and the man died as a result of the gunshot wound. I really thought wow, when will I ever get a chance again to be on a jury trial that involved a murder case?

"So when I heard the attorneys asking the other potential jurors personal questions about their past, I decided to be careful when I spoke to them. I thought if I was careful I would increase my odds of being selected on the panel.

"When the attorneys called juror number 6, my standard response was 'Not that I am aware of,' regarding every question they asked me about violence in my immediate family. I said either 'No' or pleasantly said, 'Not that I am aware of, sir.' It was not difficult to figure out how to answer the questions. Between both attorneys and their questions, the answering portion took me less than five minutes to complete."

Ricky was amazed by what he was hearing from his wife – that in a matter of moments she had decided to deceive everyone involved in the court case. He was astonished at her explanation of how easy it was for her to falsify her testimony, and how she had lied and manipulated the system to increase her chances of being involved in the trial.

Julie had wanted to hear the truth from Mary, but she was not prepared for what she heard, either. She would never have thought her daughter was capable of this level of deception. Both Julie and Ricky kept quiet and continued to listen to Mary share what was in her mind and on her heart.

Mary said, "When I learned I was, in fact, selected, I was very excited. I knew what I did was wrong, but the excitement of being involved in a murder trial outweighed the small details of information that I did not disclose to the judge or the attorneys about my past.

"On my way home, I started to think how I was going to answer the questions that Ricky would surely have for me. I knew he would ask how I was able to sit in the jury panel box overseeing a murder trial. My plan was to be very vague, and I mentioned to him that the judge did not want us speaking to anyone about the trial, including our spouses.

"After the kids were in bed, Ricky started to tell me that he could not understand how the judge or the attorneys would allow me on the case. Ricky would not drop the subject. He knew something was not right, and that is when I decided to not tell him the truth. I figured the only way to get him to stop questioning me was to tell him a small lie that he could not prove was a lie. Ricky thought and felt something was not right that night, but he could not prove that I was not telling him the truth.

"The next morning the trial began, and I got what I wanted, which was to be on a murder trial. Ricky didn't ask me any more questions because he respected the fact that the judge told the jurors not to discuss the case with anyone. Ricky had been a juror before so he knew the judge told jurors to avoid the temptation of telling their spouse what they thought about a witness or about the case in general."

Ricky looked at Julie, and Julie looked at Ricky. Anticipating that Ricky would not be able to let Mary's deceit go unanswered, Julie waited for an angry outburst. Not only had Mary confessed to lying to her husband, she seemed to feel the deception was justified because she obtained her desired outcome.

Running his fingers through his hair in frustration, Ricky did not respond with words. Instead, he took a deep breath as tears rolled down his cheeks. Julie thought that her son-in-law was showing a remarkable level of restraint.

She knew Ricky was a Godly man and that he was the main reason her daughter had come to Christ many years ago and his children studied the Bible at their church. Julie knew that Ricky's heart was being torn apart at hearing what his wife had done, and that she seemingly had no remorse for her decisions to deceive everyone, especially him.

Mary continued her story. "When the trial actually began, and I was looking at the defendant all dressed up like he was from Wall Street, I just got a bad feeling about him. The prosecuting attorney did bring to our attention the fact that at the time of his arrest, the defendant had much longer hair, as well as facial hair.

"When I heard the testimony of that worthless driver of the car that night while he was in the witness stand, I figured they were two peas in a pod. I continued to listen to the other witnesses, but I kept staring at the defendant sitting in his chair, knowing that he admittedly pulled the trigger that killed a man.

"As the trial continued, I found myself getting angrier with the defendant. I was wondering if he was possibly one of the guys in the parking lot of the movie theater where Andy was shot. It would not have surprised me in the least to learn that the defendant had been involved in many other dangerous and possibly deadly situations. Perhaps this was not the first time he pulled the trigger and released a bullet that struck someone dead.

"I just knew deep in my heart that this man was guilty of so much more than what was being discussed at this trial. I wished I could see into his mind to find what damage he has caused other families. I decided right then and there, that this man needed to go to jail so that other law-abiding citizens would not have to be hurt by him in the future."

Again, Julie looked at Ricky, and Ricky looked at Julie. Both of them had just heard Mary admit that she didn't care what evidence was presented at the trial. She had decided that she would be the one responsible for sending the defendant to jail, no matter what the other jury members thought. And, from her self-righteous tone, it was obvious that Mary did not think she had done anything wrong. The more Mary told Ricky and Julie, the worse the story became.

Mary said, "While the jury panel was in the deliberation room discussing the evidence, the testimonies, and the charges that were filed against the defendant, I concocted a plan to make sure the defendant would be forced to stay in jail for a long time. That is when I said Paulson stopped fearing for his life and decided he wanted revenge on Candlestick because he pointed the plastic gun in his face and tried to take his money. If Paulson was acting out of revenge, then the voluntary manslaughter charge would fit the crime, and no one could dispute what I felt to be true.

"My judgment was based on my perceptions of Paulson as a murderer. That is how I was able to keep a thug off the streets of Atlanta and perhaps save someone else's brother from getting killed by a stray bullet."

Looking earnestly at her mother and husband, Mary said, "Now remember what you said before regarding if I told you the truth. You promised that you weren't going to stop loving me, and I am going to hold you to your promises."

It seemed Mary wanted them both to thank her and congratulate her for thinking of a way to punish the defendant. Ricky couldn't help but wonder what else his wife was capable of doing. Mary had deceived so many people in the past seven days, but the biggest deception lay within her.

Now, a man was in jail because of the way his wife viewed him with her haughty eyes. Ricky reflected on the sermon his family had attended just the day before. He thought about the Golden Rule mentioned in the book of Matthew in chapter 7. The terms "hypocrisy" and "counterfeit Christian" were suddenly bouncing around in his mind. Ricky thought about the parable of the farmer scattering seeds and the different types of people the seeds represented.

Ricky also thought about the seven things that God detests: haughty eyes, a lying tongue, hands that kill the innocent, a heart that plots evil, feet that race to do wrong, a false witness who pours out lies, and a person who sows discord in a family. He thought about how people treat their brothers and sisters, and about how people take their deeds and their works here on earth with them when they face God on the Day of Judgment.

He thought about eternity, and he thought about heaven and hell. He wondered what his true standing was with God. He asked himself if Satan was involved in this scenario that had been revealed to him by his wife. Ricky's mind was racing, and he was distraught that the person closest to him could deceive him so easily.

Ricky knew he was caught up in something that would not be fixed this evening. He and his mother-in-law would have to pray about how to respond to Mary's actions and not just react out of emotion. He also had to consider the promise that he had made to his wife before she confessed her deeds.

Ricky also had to think about his two beautiful children and the impact the decisions Mary had made recently would have on them. He might have to reach out to some professionals, as well as his pastor, for help.

Ricky asked himself one final question: Am I caught up in a spiritual battle of good and evil, or is this simply a case where someone died and someone had to pay?

My fellow jurors and I received this letter via the Gwinnett County Court approximately two weeks after the trial was completed. I've included it here in its entirety, minus the defendant's signature.

Dear Jurors,

I've wrestled with the appropriateness of this for a few weeks, but I have decided to go with my heart. First I would like to thank you all for takeing the time out of your lives to sit on my jury. I also want to apologize for any inconveniences you may have went through because of the length of my trial. I want to thank you all for your careful examination of the facts in my case. Also your diligent deliberations when the time came to make your decision on my fate. Your unanimous decisions have given me a chance to one day return to my family and to society. I thank you from the bottom of my heart for that opportunity. Although my release will not be immediate I am confident that it will be soon. You as an independent juror and a collective jury made that possible. Words will never be able to express the gratitude that I feel. I do not want to impede your life anymore than I already have. But, I felt it absolutely necessary to thank you all personally for the time you gave out of your lives to deliberate my case and ultimately making a decision that will return my life to me. Thank you again from the bottom of my heart and God bless!

Sincerely,

Chapter 16

Fair and Impartial

purposefully did not resolve the dilemma for you between Mary and her husband. All of their dialogue – as well as the scenario involving the murder of Mary's younger brother – came from my imagination. I don't know what Mary's true motivations were in insisting on a voluntary manslaughter verdict, but obviously her previous experiences shaped her view of the world and played a part in what happened in the injustice that occurred in that courtroom.

As I mentioned in Chapter One, I was recently interviewed by CBS46 in Atlanta as well as a digital news outlet called Patch.com regarding the Justin Ross Harris trial. In April 2016, the presiding judge reluctantly granted a motion to relocate that trial because the legal teams were not able to find enough citizens who could be considered fair and impartial and who could serve on the jury.

The case, which has received a great deal of national media attention, was being tried to determine if Harris intentionally left his 22-month-old son to die in the back seat of his car during a hot day in Atlanta. Harris claims he forgot to drop his child off at daycare and was unaware that the boy was still strapped in his car seat when he went to work.

According to local news outlets, the court planned to qualify 42 prospective jurors and then whittle that total down to the final 12, plus four alternates. Three hundred and seventy-five citizens were summoned, and 250 of them appeared in court.

Through the *voir dire* process, the court decides which citizens qualify for jury duty and which citizens will be released from their obligation for cause. Cause occurs when prospective jurors display bias or prejudice related to the trial for which they are being considered.

In the Harris case, each citizen in the jury pool was asked to complete a 17-page questionnaire. The prospective jurors were told the questionnaire was not meant to be intrusive. Instead, the court said, the questionnaire was an important means to ensure that a fair and impartial jury was selected to hear and decide the case.

As the prospective jurors filled out the questionnaire, the court explained that honesty and candor were of the utmost importance. The local citizens were reminded that they had taken an oath promising to give truthful answers. The integrity of the process depended upon their truthfulness.

The court was saying, then, that the legal system relies on the citizens of the United States of America to be honest and truthful, and to possess integrity. If our citizens do not possess these characteristics, then the court's attempt to have a fair and impartial jury presiding over the case of a fellow human being may not be possible. If the legal process is flawed, it is due to the fact that the character of citizens is flawed. Unfortunately, in the Harris case, the *voir dire* process was terminated by the judge after three weeks of intense interviews of the 250 local citizens.

In my discussions with the media I explained in part, "The pursuit of fairness and justice is honorable and desired by most citizens. But what could possibly be fair about a 22-month-old boy dying in a hot car? Balancing the scales of justice is no easy task because people bring their education, or the lack thereof, their life experiences, their biases and prejudices into the courtroom. What person can check their feelings in at the door like a hat and coat and not feel compassion or anger about a precious child not being able to grow up to become an adult?"

With that being said, one potential juror supposedly said, "I hope he rots in hell." Other candidates for the jury stated they believed Harris was guilty. As a reminder, they made their decision of guilt after hearing media reports – but before reviewing any official evidence that would have been accepted by the court. Other citizens who were in the juror pool said they believed that the defense attorney would have to prove to them that Harris was not guilty of intentionally leaving his son in the back seat of his car to die.

Have we forgotten, or perhaps some of us have never been taught; that American citizens have fought and died for the legal concept of presumption of innocence until proven guilty. In fact, one reason we fought the King of England in the Revolutionary War was because concerned people living in this country didn't agree with the legal system promoted by the crown.

Back then, the King of England could publicly declare that if a person didn't pay his taxes, he was guilty of treason. For example, if I lived during that time, and the King accused me of treason because of unpaid taxes, word would spread quickly. All of my neighbors and the people I worked with would hear that I was guilty of treason. The news of my guilt would travel through the schools, and my children would be treated harshly because of the King's public declaration of my guilt.

Suddenly, my family's lives would be turned upside down. After many beatings, my children would stop going to school. Former friends of theirs would turn on them in hatred, cursing my children and calling them sons and daughters of a traitor.

My wife would lose her job because the public declaration by the King of England would have spread across our city like an uncontrollable wild fire that destroys thousands of acres of dried forest lands. Local businesses would decide not to sell or exchange goods with her because of my new reputation as a traitor. Within days, my family would have run out of food and have limited options for survival.

Meanwhile, I would be sitting, bloodied and bruised, in a filthy jail cell.

Continuing this scenario, what if eight days later, the King's accountant realized he had made an error in his journal? The accountant would explain to the King that the money due for taxes from Terry Rathmann was inadvertently credited to another citizen's account.

The accountant would tell the King that he was sorry about this honest mistake, and he also would tell the King that he would be happy to help clear the name of Terry Rathmann as a traitor to his government.

That same afternoon, the King of England would send out another public declaration stating that Terry Rathmann was not a traitor, and that he had faithfully paid his taxes every year. The King would explain to the citizens that there was an accounting error, and the error had been corrected. As a result, I would be released from jail and would be free to go on with my life with my family.

But, just because the King corrected the mistake, would my reputation be restored as it once was prior to being charged as a traitor? Would the reputations of my wife and children be restored immediately and fully?

Do you agree that my reputation and status in my city and country would have been tarnished forever? That is exactly the scenario that Thomas Jefferson fought to prevent as he declared that in the United States of America, citizens would be thought of as innocent until proven guilty. That is why a grand jury is appointed to review the evidence and make a determination if charges should even be brought to trial.

My example may seem extreme, but I hope you can visualize the dangers of not looking at a fellow human being as innocent until proven guilty. Take that one step further to the golden rule found in the Book of Matthew 7:12: *"Do to others whatever you would like them to do to you. This is the essence of all that is taught in the law and the prophets."*

If we learn this philosophy early, it can literally change our view of the world for the rest of our lives. For instance, children should be taught at a young age about the dangers of gossip and spreading rumors. One way to illustrate this point with your children is to take a feather pillow to their school's play yard, with the permission of the school, of course. Have your children open the pillow and empty it of all its feathers, releasing them into the wind one handful at a time.

The next day, take your children and the empty pillowcase back to the play yard. Try to find all of the feathers and return them to the pillow. Your children will soon realize it is impossible to recapture all of the feathers, and that the pillow is now only a semblance of what it was.

The feathers can represent a rumor or story about a classmate. Ask your children how they could possibly verify if a story they were told at school about a classmate was true. By discussing what effort it could take to find the truth, your children might realize that – like finding all the feathers – determining the truth could be impossible. Explain to your children that when someone tells them a story or a rumor, and they then tell another classmate, and that student then tells someone else, a story is flying around the school like the feathers were flying around in the school yard.

If the feathers represent the rumor, the pillowcase can represent the classmate who is being discussed. Because of the gossip that has been spread throughout the school, that child likely will never be the same. By sharing the rumor, your children are permanently changing the emotional and physical well-being of a classmate. Just like the pillow was never able to be filled with all of the original feathers, the classmate will not ever fully be put back together. Finally, remind your children that whoever gossips with them will also gossip about them. Teach your children what you likely were taught many years ago: If you can't say anything nice, then don't say anything at all.

Take this scenario back to the Justin Ross Harris and Darren Paulson trials. What can we learn about the character of an individual, a city, a county, or a nation when the citizens cannot bring it upon themselves to look at a human being as innocent until proven guilty? Why would a person jump to a conclusion about another? Why would a citizen, without a single piece of evidence, continue to spread a rumor – a story that might or might not be true – about another citizen? Having a gut feeling about something or someone does not qualify as a legal method of eliminating uncertainty.

With that being said, how do we enhance our character so that honesty, truthfulness and integrity are the overwhelming characteristics that guide our lives here on earth? I believe there are two standards that we can adopt for our lives.

Too often, our culture seems to encourage us to place our personal desires above all else. While our cultural standards are always changing, self-centeredness prevails. Unfortunately, within this environment it is difficult to find people who can put aside their own preconceived ideas and be fair and impartial.

The ideal juror, however, must follow the values of honesty, truthfulness and integrity. Many religions, including my Christian faith, share these values. Out of love for His creation, God gave Moses the 10 commandments. These commandments should be considered standards on how human beings should treat God, and each other.

For instance, God tells us not to be a false witness or a liar, not to murder, and not to commit adultery. God tells us not to steal and not to be jealous of a neighbor's possessions. God tells us to honor our mothers and our earthly fathers. God tells us not to worship anything or anyone above Him.

Imagine the impact on our court system if we accepted and followed these standards of living. We wouldn't have nearly as many cases to try, and it would be simple to find a fair and impartial juror panel to review charges brought against others.

We all have two options. We can trust the standards of our culture and choose to be self-centered, or we can trust God, and live by the values and standards written in the Bible that our loving God gave us thousands of years ago. Those values – shared by many other religions and even by people who don't practice a religion at all – should be the foundation of our democracy, and our court system.

We often hear in the news about the need to have separation of church and state. Perhaps, too, we need to discuss having separation of culture and state. The standards of a culture should not dictate laws to be created and followed by American citizens.

God gave us standards not to limit our joy while on earth, but to enhance our joy knowing that our hearts would not be contaminated in the pursuit of our personal desires. God gave us these standards because as every loving Father should, He wants the very best for us. Living by these standards will allow us to have an awesome loving relationship with each other, and with our Heavenly Father, God Almighty.

Can you look at someone and declare they are innocent until proven guilty? If not, how can you change your mind and heart so that you can enact the golden rule in your life? If you could choose, would you want your children to live in a world that looked upon them as being innocent until proven guilty?

I leave you with two final questions. What are you willing to do for yourself, for your family, your parents, and your fellow citizens and human beings, in order to commit yourself to being a fair and impartial person? Which values and standards will you choose to live by, and which will you promote to the people who surround you?

Take the Juror 11 Pledge

 PLEDGE allegiance to each citizen of the United States of America by agreeing to be a fair-minded and impartial citizen. I PLEDGE to look upon each individual as being innocent, until the facts are presented beyond a reasonable doubt that proves guilt. I PLEDGE to all American citizens that my pursuit of liberty, happiness, wealth, and personal justice, will not come at the expense of an individual, a gender or a race. I PLEDGE that I will not allow my family background, whether privileged or not, to tilt the scales of justice by ignoring what is right and wrong. I PLEDGE to all American citizens that I will spend my time here on earth attempting to construct a nation that is second to none. I PLEDGE to strive daily to bring honor to the men and women who sacrificed their lives serving something larger than themselves. I PLEDGE Allegiance to the flag of the United States of America and to the republic for which it stands, one nation, under God, indivisible, with liberty and justice for all.

Signature: _____

Date: _____

About the Author

Both sets of grandparents were farmers in Minnesota

Served in the United States Army infantry

Majored in political science and minored in business administration

Formerly an account executive for Turner Broadcasting Systems

Formerly a senior area sales manager for DIRECTV

Founded Worldly Concepts, a sales and marketing
consulting firm, in 2000

Founded Direct Satellite TV, which Terry and Lynda still
operate today, in 2005

Founded A SHEPHERD'S LIFE 7 INC. 501(c) (3) in 2015

A Shepherd's Life is a non-profit video Bible study ministry. Our mission is to lead people to study God's word, chapter by chapter, verse by verse, so that everyone can understand what God has done for us in the past, and how He is working in our present and preparing us for His future.

Leaders are needed in today's world. We ask God to send us the Spirit of Wisdom as we study his word, so that we can become wise shepherds for our families, our churches, our professions and the communities in which we live. Amen!

A new video is released every week and we include additional written questions per lesson for those who want to dig a little deeper into God's word @ www.ashepherdslife.org

CPSIA information can be obtained at www.ICGtesting.com
Printed in the USA
LVOW10s0151310816

502447LV00002B/3/P